An obsession that cannot die . . .

Bantam Books in the Sweet Valley University series.
Ask your bookseller for the books you have missed.

#1 COLLEGE GIRLS
#2 LOVE, LIES, AND JESSICA WAKEFIELD
#3 WHAT YOUR PARENTS DON'T KNOW . . .
#4 ANYTHING FOR LOVE
#5 A MARRIED WOMAN
#6 THE LOVE OF HER LIFE
#7 GOOD-BYE TO LOVE
#8 HOME FOR CHRISTMAS
#9 SORORITY SCANDAL
#10 NO MEANS NO
#11 TAKE BACK THE NIGHT
#12 COLLEGE CRUISE
#13 SS HEARTBREAK
#14 SHIPBOARD WEDDING
#15 BEHIND CLOSED DOORS
#16 THE OTHER WOMAN
#17 DEADLY ATTRACTION
#18 BILLIE'S SECRET
#19 BROKEN PROMISES, SHATTERED DREAMS
#20 HERE COMES THE BRIDE
#21 FOR THE LOVE OF RYAN
#22 ELIZABETH'S SUMMER LOVE
#23 SWEET KISS OF SUMMER
#24 HIS SECRET PAST
#25 BUSTED!
#26 THE TRIAL OF JESSICA WAKEFIELD
#27 ELIZABETH AND TODD FOREVER
#28 ELIZABETH'S HEARTBREAK
#29 ONE LAST KISS
#30 BEAUTY AND THE BEACH
#31 THE TRUTH ABOUT RYAN
#32 THE BOYS OF SUMMER
#33 OUT OF THE PICTURE
#34 SPY GIRL
#35 UNDERCOVER ANGELS
#36 HAVE YOU HEARD ABOUT ELIZABETH?
#37 BREAKING AWAY
#38 GOOD-BYE, ELIZABETH
#39 ELIZABETH ♥ NEW YORK
#40 PRIVATE JESSICA
#41 ESCAPE TO NEW YORK
#42 SNEAKING IN
#43 THE PRICE OF LOVE
#44 LOVE ME ALWAYS

And don't miss these Sweet Valley University Thriller Editions:

#1 WANTED FOR MURDER
#2 HE'S WATCHING YOU
#3 KISS OF THE VAMPIRE
#4 THE HOUSE OF DEATH
#5 RUNNING FOR HER LIFE
#6 THE ROOMMATE
#7 WHAT WINSTON SAW
#8 DEAD BEFORE DAWN
#9 KILLER AT SEA
#10 CHANNEL X
#11 LOVE AND MURDER
#12 DON'T ANSWER THE PHONE
#13 CYBERSTALKER: THE RETURN OF WILLIAM WHITE, PART I

Visit the Official Sweet Valley Web Site on the Internet at:

http://www.sweetvalley.com

SWEET VALLEY UNIVERSITY®

THRILLER EDITION

CyberStalker:

The Return of William White, Part I

Written by
Laurie John

Created by
FRANCINE PASCAL

BANTAM BOOKS
NEW YORK • TORONTO • LONDON • SYDNEY • AUCKLAND

RL 8, age 14 and up

CYBERSTALKER: THE RETURN OF WILLIAM WHITE, PART I
A Bantam Book / January 1999

*Produced by 17th Street Productions,
a division of Daniel Weiss Associates, Inc.
33 West 17th Street
New York, NY 10011.*

ISBN: 0-553-49227-6

Published simultaneously in the United States and Canada

Bantam Books are published by Bantam Books, a division of Random House, Inc. Its trademark, consisting of the words "Bantam Books" and the portrayal of a rooster, is Registered in U.S. Patent and Trademark Office and in other countries. Marca Registrada. Bantam Books, 1540 Broadway, New York, New York 10036.

PRINTED IN THE UNITED STATES OF AMERICA

OPM 0 9 8 7 6 5 4 3 2 1

To Alexandra Nicole Petrucci

Chapter One

"I thought my Friday lab was going to go on for-*ever*," Elizabeth Wakefield complained as she flopped down onto the futon couch inside room 28, Dickenson Hall. "Whew! I'm dying for a little R and R." With a cathartic sigh she turned and smiled at her boyfriend, Tom Watts.

Tom stood in the dorm room's small kitch-enette and poured tea into two mugs. "Well, you can rule out any plans for the beach this week-end," he replied. He furrowed his brow as he looked out the window.

Elizabeth followed Tom's gaze. Beyond the trees outside, a thick, purplish black band of clouds loomed. She had never seen anything quite like it before. She turned away from the window when Tom handed her a mug of tea. Chamomile, her favorite.

"I can't believe we're not going to get any rain

from this front," Tom added with a shake of his head. "The WSVU weather guys are usually pretty accurate. I guess we'll just have to wait and see."

Elizabeth sipped her tea and frowned. It *was* pretty bizarre. All day, every weather report she'd heard foretold a sudden change of weather—dark, heavy storm clouds that seemed to come out of nowhere—yet supposedly there was no threat of rain.

Hard to believe, she mused as her eyes followed the menacing band of black striping the horizon. Even more hard to believe was the fact that she was sitting in her dorm room with Tom, discussing the weather for the fourth time today as if they were an old married couple. Could things get any more boring between them?

Elizabeth sighed and stole a look at her boyfriend. His warm brown eyes reflected none of the concern Elizabeth was feeling. In fact, Tom didn't even register Elizabeth's gaze. He was already settled comfortably on the floor, his back against Elizabeth's bed. A pen between his teeth, he flipped through a calculus textbook.

A calculus textbook!

She sighed again, louder this time, just to see if Tom would react. He didn't so much as move a muscle until he snatched the pen from his mouth to scribble something in the margin of his text.

Elizabeth bit her lip and turned away from the sight of him. *Dull, dull, dull!* she thought angrily. Couples in nursing homes had wilder times than they did. And for all Tom seemed to care, Elizabeth might as well have been a lab rat, a pile of clay, or a coat hanger. So long as she blurted out the occasional monosyllable, Tom wouldn't even notice the difference.

Not that things had always been that way. Elizabeth smiled wistfully as she remembered the way she and Tom had once felt around each other. Forget electric shocks—the first time she and Tom had ever danced together, Elizabeth thought she'd melt faster than a candle in an active volcano. But lately things had grown a little stale. No, *worse* than stale—they were positively flat-lining.

Elizabeth picked at a loose thread of her turquoise cotton sweater. Familiarity was one thing, she reasoned, but there was a pretty big difference between relationship comfort zone and relationship coma. She knew that all too well now.

She twisted the blue thread in her forefinger and yanked it without thinking. With an odd sense of detachment she watched the edge of her sweater seam begin to unravel.

Like our relationship . . .

Elizabeth hurriedly tossed the thought from her mind. Why couldn't she just be positive for once? At the very least, she figured, she could *act* positive. Maybe then Tom would finally come around and stop behaving like a stagnating old bore.

Forcing a sweet smile to her lips, she turned

back around to look at her boyfriend. She let her eyes settle on Tom's handsome face. The clean planes of his cheekbones and angular jaw were illuminated by the afternoon light, gray and gloomy though it might be.

Just because you're in a slump doesn't mean it's the end, she resolved. The thought cheered her up enough to relax her smile. Just then Tom closed his calculus book and stuffed his pen in his pocket. A good sign, Elizabeth knew. Because it seemed as if lately Tom had spent more time studying than even *she* had. And everyone on the campus of Sweet Valley University—including Elizabeth herself—knew she was renowned for perpetually having her nose in one book or another.

"Hey, let's do something different this weekend," Elizabeth suggested. "The beach may be out of commission, but gloomy nights are great for black-and-white video marathons. Let's rent *Casablanca* and a couple of Hitchcocks—*Rebecca* . . . or maybe *Dial M for Murder*. . . ."

"I've seen those," Tom replied idly. He glanced out the window again as the charcoal clouds advanced. They looked as if they were stalking slowly toward campus, like a beast toward its prey.

Elizabeth scowled, her mood darkening once again. "I *know* you've seen those movies already, Tom," she snapped. Wasn't that the whole point? Part of the charm of rewatching old movies was knowing what was going to come next. Not to mention having someone to snuggle up with and share in the fun.

So much for rekindling the romance, Elizabeth thought morosely. Her twin sister, Jessica, had complained time and time again that Tom Watts was a drag and a half. Elizabeth would always defend Tom to the end. But right now Tom wasn't doing much to prove Jessica wrong.

Elizabeth wondered what Jessica would say if she could hear the conversation that had just taken place. A half smile played at the corners of Elizabeth's mouth as she pictured her twin rolling her eyes and shaking her head in amazement. "You might as well be dating a corpse!" Jessica would say in disgust. She'd said it before, plenty of times.

Maybe I'd be better off dating a corpse, Elizabeth thought sourly. At least a dead guy wouldn't argue with her all the time. And a dead guy wouldn't make her miserable with his moodiness, his temper, his constant complaining. . . .

She mentally shook the thought away. Jessica's opinions on romance—whether they involved corpses or not—were hardly any basis for gauging the strength of a relationship. Although the twins were identical, from their blue-green eyes and thick, long blond hair to the dimples in their left cheeks, they marched to very different drums. Jessica lived for thrills and excitement, getting herself into all sorts of trouble, while Elizabeth took life more seriously, preferring study to spontaneity and practical reality to a world of fantasy, fashion, and flirting.

No, Elizabeth decided as her gaze rested on Tom's broad shoulders and taut, muscled biceps, displayed to perfection by his black pocket T. She would much rather be rooted in routine with Tom than have a Jessica-style relationship any day. Elizabeth and Tom's love had a good, solid foundation. They had gone through a lot together and had always found a way to survive. Maybe the fireworks weren't blazing between them like they used to, but at least they could count on each other.

That's what really matters, Elizabeth thought. Sure, things could use a little kick, but that wouldn't be hard to arrange. Every relationship went through its valleys now and then, but it was nothing a little time and effort couldn't fix.

"So what do you suggest for this weekend?" Elizabeth purred, flashing Tom a sultry look. If that wasn't an obvious hint for a candlelight dinner at Andre's, then she didn't know what was.

"We could . . . study?" Tom suggested, drumming his fingers on the pile of books to his side. "You've got that art history exam coming up. And if I don't get my head around the maxima and minima of definite integrals, I'm going to have to find a new way to fulfill my core requirements. . . ."

As Tom chattered on, Elizabeth sat stone-faced. *Studying!* Of course Elizabeth liked to study, and nobody ever had to drag her to the library. But couldn't Tom see that this was one weekend when studying was *not* on Elizabeth's list of priorities?

Miserable, Elizabeth stood up and walked over to the window. *How can two people who are so close be so far away from each other?* she wondered, a hollow feeling expanding in her stomach as she peeked through the blinds. At that moment an eerie reddish maroon glow emanated from the center of the stripe of clouds nearing campus. Just as quickly as it appeared, the glow dimmed and died. Elizabeth shivered as the clouds thickened, obliterating whatever was left of the grayish sunlight.

The hollow in Elizabeth's stomach grew into a dark pit. *Just like the sky,* she thought. As she watched the bad weather approaching, Elizabeth felt gloom seep into her very bones. And something else too. Something ominous.

She turned away from the window and tried to force all unhappy thoughts from her mind. But it was no use. A rumble from somewhere beyond the horizon echoed and then stilled, as if in answer to Elizabeth's silent questions.

Elizabeth dropped the blind and left the room. She could no longer look at Tom, and most of all she could no longer look at the bruised sky. It was too much of an omen, foretelling the death of their love.

* * *

"Well, as far as I'm concerned, if they could put one man on the moon, then why not all of them?" Jessica tossed her hair impetuously. "They're all a bunch of freaks. At least two rungs lower down on the evolutionary scale than women."

"Is this *Invasion of the Body Snatchers, Part Four*?" Lila Fowler asked. She studied her friend, narrowing her large brown eyes. "I mean, there's no way the Jessica Wakefield *I* know would *ever* say something so sacrilegious."

"Must be," Jessica agreed, "because there's no way the Lila Fowler *I* know would *ever* use a word like *sacrilegious.* I thought the biggest word you knew was *espadrilles.*"

"Look, let's get back to *my* point, OK?" Lila flipped her thick mane of chestnut hair over her shoulder. "I don't know what's come over you, Jessica, I really don't. This new antimale attitude of yours has me a bit concerned. Actually," she added with a snort of derision, "I'm not *really* concerned. There's no way it will last. Jessica Wakefield without someone to lust after is like Barbie without accessories. It just isn't marketable."

Jessica adjusted the strap of the red patent-leather book bag on her shoulder. "Maybe. But honestly, what can I do? I've had it with the whole male species. They're biologically inferior, with a built-in mechanism for deception. And they don't come with a warranty card either. When they don't work, you can't exchange them . . . not immediately anyway. Not without a lot of hassle."

"You're just saying that because you've picked a handful of defects," Lila said as they approached the quad. A whistling wind blew a leaf into her carefully styled coif. "Jeez! What's up with this weather?"

"It's pretty weird for this time of year." Jessica shivered in her thin georgette dress. Anxiously she watched a funnel of wind create a minitornado from a pile of dust. She raised her hands in a protective shield over her hair.

"If you're so *not* up for meeting men, then why, pray tell, bother guarding the 'do?" Lila scoffed as they dodged the dust tornado.

"Lila," Jessica began wearily, "I don't dress for men. I dress for *me*."

"Yeah, right," Lila drawled. "And my father's the poorest man in Sweet Valley."

Jessica rolled her eyes as they crossed the windy quad. Lila could be so annoying sometimes! It was bad enough having a best friend who spent her life basking in the glow of her rich daddy's bank account. But that wasn't nearly as much of a problem as Lila's obvious lack of depth. She could be so unbelievably superficial. Hadn't Lila heard that they were on the threshold of the twenty-first century? Hadn't she heard that it was possible for women to live without men? From the way Lila acted, Jessica was surprised she didn't refer to cars as "horseless carriages."

What's the point anyway? Jessica asked herself. Until a man worthy of her time and energy came her way, she wasn't going to strain herself, and she wasn't going to rush into anything stupid. She'd be single and loving it.

Just then a cute, well-muscled guy with thick brown hair and full lips passed by. He gave Jessica a broad smile. Almost automatically, Jessica smiled back demurely. *Not half bad,* she found herself thinking.

"Who was that?" Lila asked. She cast a look of approval at the disappearing stranger.

"Just some silly freshman admirer," Jessica replied, affecting a tone of boredom. "Nothing to rock my world."

"You're definitely not yourself, Jess." Lila shook her head as if the stock market had just collapsed. "I mean, I'm all for being picky, but you don't have to go to extremes."

Jessica sighed. Naturally Lila couldn't understand where she was coming from. Lila spent her life in a silk designer cocoon. What did she know of the intricacies of love and betrayal? Jessica, on the other hand, had spent her years being ruled by her foolish heart, falling in love without so much as blinking, rushing from one disaster into another, and all because she trusted.

Blindly! she reminded herself. It was about time she grew up. All the things Elizabeth had said to her over the years, all the things that she,

Jessica, had scoffed at, suddenly came at her like a million babbling brooks of wisdom.

Look before you leap!

If it feels too good to be true, it is too good to be true!

Out of the frying pan into the fire!

Elizabeth was right, even though Jessica wasn't about to admit it to her face anytime soon. Sometimes it *was* better to be safe than sorry. Of course, getting involved with a boring old toad like Tom Watts would be taking safety a little too far.

Still, Jessica was out for something genuine, something real. Something nice and comfortable with someone she could trust.

And I will find it, Jessica told herself. No matter how long she had to wait, she would *not* compromise. Even if it took forever. Even if she died trying.

"Sorry, Jess, but I simply can't share your enthusiasm for the single life," Lila said as she and Jessica dashed out of the Red Lion, each gripping a Mochaccino to go. A dreamy smile played on the corners of Lila's glossy lips. Peach Glace, the newest color by Dora of Milan. Lila had arranged for it to be sent straight from Italy to her door, securing that important one-month jump on the more trend-conscious—but less well connected—California makeup mavens.

Her boyfriend, Bruce Patman, had told her the

color looked as if it had been made just for her. Then again, he said that about *everything* she wore. That was precisely what made them so blissfully compatible.

Bruce was, in Lila's eyes, simply nature's most perfect creation. Not only did he have shoulders broad enough to run a marathon on—which, paired with his seductive slate blue eyes and shiny, always perfect dark hair, made him the catch of SVU if not the entire West Coast—well, on top of all that, he possessed every single one of the qualities and values that Lila most respected and admired in a man. The values instilled in her by her parents. The crucial elements needed to fortify and till the soil of any meaningful relationship.

Bruce had money. Lots of it.

Not that money itself was all-important to Lila. She wasn't *that* superficial. No, the importance of money was that it gave a man a chance to show how generous he was. In Bruce's case, his Multinational Express UltraPlatinum card gave him every opportunity to prove to Lila just how much he loved and appreciated her.

Of course, if Bruce hadn't been so keen on lavishing dinners and expensive Tiffany bracelets on her, her daddy most certainly would have filled in the gaps. But luckily it hadn't come to that. Bruce was only too thrilled to pick up the tab; naturally Lila was only too pleased to accept his adoration. Their relationship couldn't have been more perfect.

As Lila began recounting the details of a slew of romantic purchases Bruce had recently made for her, Jessica let out a snort.

"Give me a break, Li," Jessica snarled, her complexion going all ruddy. "Life is not a string of Cartier pearls, in case you haven't noticed. What would happen if the Patmans lost all their money in some freak stock-market crash?"

"What?" Lila gasped. "That would never happen. I mean, how dare you even *suggest* such a thing? I can't believe you'd say something so . . . morbid!" Lila shivered at the thought of Bruce, a broken man, walking the streets in pedestrian Calvin Klein jeans instead of his custom-made Italian silk pants. As this nasty image broke into Lila's thoughts, a dark, ominous shadow fell across the quad. She looked up to see a huge puff of a blue-black cloud sailing above her head. The timing was unsettling. Could Jessica have made a prediction about Bruce's financial future?

Suddenly a white-hot bolt of lightning scissored out from the nest of dark clouds and shot down to earth, as if confirming Lila's worst fears. But just as Lila was about to open her mouth and tell Jessica what was going through her mind, her gaze darted over toward where the bolt had struck ground. A huge, white tent stood silent as a ghost at the far end of the quad, eerily backlit as if it had captured the lightning and held it within. Menacing thunderclaps resonated through the air.

"Where did that come from?" Jessica whispered.

"Beats me," Lila replied. The tent was huge and appeared to be glowing a frothy white, like a stray cloud that had accidentally blown down from the morning sky and landed in the quad to shelter from the storm.

"It's way creepy looking," Jessica breathed. She clutched Lila's arm. "How come we didn't notice it before?"

"Maybe because we were too busy talking about your newfangled approach to life without men."

"If I remember correctly, we were just talking about the profound love between you and Bruce's credit card."

Lila sighed in relief. She and Jessica were bickering as usual, and the low, dark cloud had sped away, taking with it the threat of more lightning. Everything was back to normal. Except that weird tent still sat there at the far end of the quad. It was huge, about as wide as SVU's Olympic-size swimming pool and about twice as tall as the pool was deep. Curiosity replaced the last remaining twinges of fear in Lila's heart. "Want to take a peek?" she asked.

"Most definitely," Jessica replied. "Just hold on a sec." She whipped a compact from her purse and skimmed her lips with gloss in one expert swipe.

Lila grinned. "Planning on running into your

freshman admirer at the other end of the quad?" she asked, arching a perfect eyebrow knowingly.

"It never hurts to look your best." Jessica snapped the compact shut. "Now let's go check out that giant marshmallow that strayed from the flock, shall we?"

"CyberDreams Virtual Reality Fair," Lila read, her hands on her hips. "Hmmm. No signs of Freddy Krueger or Michael Myers anywhere. I wonder what the deal is?"

Jessica studied the huge arching banner that was draped in front of the mysterious white tent. "Cool logo," she noted, impressed by the large rosebud that had been expertly stitched onto the front of the tent in silver thread. "*Très* cyberstylish."

"What do you know about cyber *anything?*" Lila demanded. She stepped closer, squinting as she scrutinized the giant silver-white rosebud on the banner.

"Do you think I was born in a barn?" Jessica snapped. "I happen to have surfed the net more times than you've had your cuffs hemmed."

"Please!" Lila scoffed. "You skipped intro to computers, like, every other week."

"Oh, and I suppose *you're* the big authority on all things techno?"

"Actually, I do know a thing or two about the medium. Daddy bought me a laptop way before the things were even on the market."

"So now you're queen of the information superhighway," Jessica jibed.

"It just so happens that I ordered my entire spring wardrobe off the net," Lila responded smugly. "Plus I have an exclusive e-mail account that keeps me up-to-date on what's shipping to boutiques all over the world. From the runways of Paris straight to Lila Fowler."

Jessica rolled her eyes. Lila always thought she was one step ahead of everyone else, but this time it simply wasn't true. Granted, Jessica hadn't exactly spent much time in the chat rooms on the net—conversations with lonely old geek guys pretending to be twentysomething hotties just wasn't her thing—but she'd been to her share of raves and knew that the cyberscene wasn't limited to a bunch of nerds browsing the web. There was more to the whole techno world than that. And though Jessica didn't know all that much about virtual reality, she was willing to give anything a try.

"So is this place open or what?" Lila demanded.

"It opens tonight," Jessica replied, reading from a small sign at the door.

"It looks so weird in there." Lila poked her head around the sheeted entrance. "There aren't any lights on or anything. From the way this thing is glowing, you'd think it'd be lit up like a Christmas tree inside."

Jessica craned her neck to get a better look, but

all she could see was a main space subdivided by row after row of white sheets, an almost fluorescent white. Jessica stepped back. The contrast of the white tent against the eerie violet sky made her eyes hurt. It was like an optical illusion or something.

"There's not a soul inside," Lila commented. "But I'm sure the whole world will turn up tonight."

At the thought, Jessica felt a small thrill shoot up her spine. She'd all but resigned herself to a boring weekend, but now, unexpectedly, a potentially fun alternative had literally sprung up out of nowhere.

A delicious tremor of anticipation kicked at Jessica's insides. She could just picture the hordes of hot guys that would be crammed into the CyberDreams tent only hours from now. Sure, the place would probably be Geek Grand Central—more thick lenses and orthopedic shoes than in a retirement village. But cute boys liked video games too. . . .

Jessica smiled as she envisioned groups of gorgeous men clustered around computers or video screens or whatever idiotic guy stuff was waiting inside the tent. They'd get bored soon enough . . . and then they'd see Jessica! At that point it would be like bees to honey.

Nothing new, Jessica thought, a faraway look in her eye. *And totally harmless too.* Being surrounded by admirers was as familiar to her as brushing her teeth. And one last round of casual flirting wouldn't damage her new attitude any. It would simply be like a last hurrah—a final send-off before she blasted into the new world of singledom.

Jessica pictured cheering crowds, the kind she'd seen in movies, waving at astronauts before they boarded their waiting spaceship. She'd wear a flimsy silver gown to reflect the smiles of all the adoring men around her. Turning from the CyberDreams tent slowly but deliberately—ignoring all pleas to return—walking away into the misty night air—

"Earth to Jessica!"

Jessica blinked. "Huh?"

"Have you departed for cyberspace already?" Lila asked, waving a hand in front of her face.

"Oh, look," a horribly familiar voice drawled. "There's Jessica Wakefield, our resident space case."

Jessica wheeled around to find herself face-to-face with none other than the dreaded, beady-eyed buzz killer herself, Alison Quinn.

"Hi, Alison," Lila offered tonelessly, exchanging a secretive look of terror with Jessica.

Nice wake-up call, Jessica thought in irritation. Alison's cold, pinched face could shock anyone back to reality faster than a bucket of ice water. Still, though snotty Alison had given Jessica and Lila plenty of eye-rolling opportunities in the past, she couldn't be ignored. She was, after all, the vice president of their sorority, Theta Alpha Theta.

"Nice to see you, Alison," Jessica volunteered, trying not to sound too frosty.

"Ditto," Alison replied, drawing out the *o* so that it sounded like a long *eew.* "Planning on checking this out later?" she added, jerking her head in the direction of the tent.

"We'll be here," Jessica replied. "Oh, crud!" she added, looking at her watch in mock horror. "Lila, we're going to be late!"

Lila's eyebrows shot up. "For?"

Duh! Jessica elbowed Lila sharply. Denser than a redwood forest! "We have to go to the library," she lied pointedly.

"Library?" Lila nearly shrieked.

Make that thicker than a plank.

"It's closing soon," Jessica continued, grinding the point of her elbow into Lila's ribs. Alison simply smiled superciliously and tossed her thin, neat braid.

"Oh yes . . . uh, of course. The library," Lila stammered.

"Well, catch you later!" Alison trilled, clearly oblivious.

As Jessica and Lila hurried away from the tent, Jessica heaved a sigh of relief. Thank goodness Alison Quinn was no genius when it came to the art of communication. It would not do to get Alison's back up, no matter how pathetically freaky she was.

"You didn't have to shove me so hard," Lila whined.

"Oh yes, I did!" Jessica snapped. "Lila, you have many wonderful qualities, but you really have to learn to read the signs."

"Signs?"

Oh, boy! It was hard being mentally superior to one's own best friend. But what was a girl to do when everyone around her was so incredibly unsophisticated in the brains department? The best she could hope for was to lead her followers by example. "Don't worry, Lila," she added wearily. "Just stick with me and I'll teach you everything you need to know."

Chapter Two

That storm is nothing compared to the one right here, Elizabeth thought, touching her heart as she glanced at the angry sky above her. She had been aching for fresh air after her stale conversation with Tom, but this wasn't quite what she had in mind.

She walked briskly across the quad, barely feeling the icy wind whistling past her ears, hardly registering the somber crackling of a distant electrical storm. Her head was too full of warring voices of its own.

It's over, a little voice whispered forlornly inside her head.

No, it's not! another voice snapped.

Images of Elizabeth's relationship with Tom, past and present, vied for dominance in her mind's eye. Happy memories of romantic moonlit walks at the beach collided with the dull reality of more recent events.

"From moonlit magic to . . . monotony," Elizabeth mumbled, chuckling at her melodramatic musing. But she couldn't help herself. Maybe things really *were* dead between her and Tom. Maybe there was no point in hanging around after the funeral.

Maybe you're being a little hasty, the other, more sensible side of Elizabeth suggested. *There was once a spark between you. You simply have to reignite it.*

Lost in thought, Elizabeth continued to walk at a brisk pace, stopping only when she happened to glance up. Only then did she register what had been in front of her eyes all along.

"Whoa!" she breathed. "That's strange." The huge white tent had caught her quite by surprise. She surveyed the massive white-sheeted structure and strained her eyes to read the banner in the dying afternoon light. But before her eyes even got to the second word, they leaped, as if magnetized, to the giant white rose edged in silver.

No!

Elizabeth jumped as if she'd been branded. She closed her eyes, but the image wouldn't disappear. Instead it multiplied as if it were reflected and refracted on the inside of her eyelids. Hundreds of white rosebuds danced in her vision.

Elizabeth felt as if a cold hand were sifting through her intestines. *I'm just imagining things,* she told herself as her hands began to shake. But when she forced open her eyes, there it was again: a giant white rosebud. Just like the kind William White used to send her.

William White. Even his name sent Elizabeth into paroxysms of fear. Ever since William's deadly obsession with her, Elizabeth hadn't been able to look at a white rose in a normal way. Every time she passed a florist or spotted an arrangement in someone's dorm room, it produced the same violent reaction inside her—her stomach seized and her mouth went dry with fear. The memories would come flooding back. All those times William had pursued her, leaving behind his terrible message of twisted love—his trademark white rosebud.

At first Elizabeth had been disarmed by handsome, mysterious William. Who wouldn't have been flattered by a man who sent romantic Shakespearean sonnets accompanied by long-stemmed roses? But soon enough Elizabeth had seen the chilling truth behind the charm. William wasn't "intense"—he was psychotic, a violent sociopath with frightening fantasies. He'd led a right-wing, pseudo-fascist organization on campus, and when Elizabeth refused his advances, he'd gone completely over the edge.

But he can't hurt you now, Elizabeth reminded herself, grasping for reason and logic as the white rosebud glowed ominously on the tent. *He's dead.*

Or is he?

Suddenly Elizabeth felt a tremor of déjà vu creep up her spine, as if a ghost were playing piano on her vertebrae. Once before, Elizabeth had been positive that William was dead. After escaping from the mental institution he'd been confined to, William had crashed his car and everyone believed he was dead. But it had simply been a decoy to throw the police off his trail. He'd staged the accident and continued on his violent quest to either win Elizabeth's heart or destroy her and those she loved.

But he is *dead!* Elizabeth told herself firmly. *You saw him die with your own two eyes!*

After William's successful escape from the asylum, he'd managed to capture Elizabeth through a deft scheme of manipulation that only William could pull off. Elizabeth felt her knees quake involuntarily as she recalled the terrifying moment when she realized she was facing death head-on.

"We'll live life on our own terms—or we won't live it at all. . . ."

William's ghostly voice rang through Elizabeth's mind as clear as the ringing of a church bell at a funeral service. She bit her lip to keep her teeth from chattering, the image of his face contorted with rage swimming to the surface of her memory.

The last time she ever saw William White was as his helpless hostage in a speeding car. *Not so helpless,* Elizabeth reminded herself. By sheer force of will, knowing it was her only chance, Elizabeth had grabbed the wheel from William and tried to force the speeding car to stop. But instead of the brake, her foot had hit the gas pedal and the car had crashed in what had to have been the longest moment of Elizabeth's life.

But you survived, Elizabeth reminded herself. *You survived, and he didn't.*

Still, the memory of William's sightless eyes staring at Elizabeth as he lay slumped over the wheel of the car didn't do much to comfort her now. Nor had it comforted her then, or for months after William had met his violent end. Night after night Elizabeth had woken up in a cold sweat, William's blank eyes burning twin holes of hatred into her very soul.

"He's gone," she murmured out loud, desperate to reconvince herself. "It's a fact. William White is dead."

Forcing herself to stare at the banner in front of the tent, Elizabeth ordered herself to calm down and get a grip on reality. After a moment she even managed a nervous laugh. William White was six feet under. The white rosebud on the banner was just a coincidence. It wasn't as if the guy had a copyright on white rosebuds or anything.

After a few minutes Elizabeth felt better. She chided herself as she looked at the rosebud again. It was just an innocent white rose, stitched in silver onto an innocent white sheet. It wasn't going to stalk her, it wasn't going to hurt her, and it wasn't going to try to kill her.

Elizabeth stepped back from the tent and shook her head, banishing all thoughts of William from her mind. It was so unlike her to get worked up over nothing. How could she allow her imagination to run wild circles around her practical, fact-oriented journalist's mind?

But no matter how hard she tried to laugh off the whole William White matter, Elizabeth couldn't quite shake the feeling of unease that had settled over her like an invisible shroud.

"Get it together, girl," she told herself out loud. Obviously the oncoming storm was affecting her powers of perception. Nothing a cup of hot chocolate and a long shower couldn't fix. Pulling up the collar of her denim jacket, she made her way back toward Dickenson Hall. She'd done enough thinking for one day.

"But that's barbaric!" Lila spluttered, a forkful of creamy risotto shaking in her hand. "Locking pledges into a closet and then setting it on fire? What kind of fraternity do you belong to anyway?"

"Whoa, Li, you're not listening!" Bruce replied. "We didn't *really* set the closet on fire—we just *told* them we had. All we did was push a pot of smoking newspapers by the door and they totally freaked! It was so cool!"

"Waiter!" Lila snapped. "I need some water here. Make it a full carafe this time. I need to hydrate. So," she added, pointing a perfectly manicured finger at

Bruce, "are you telling me you've turned into some kind of pyromaniac?"

Bruce grinned and let his gaze roam lazily over his girlfriend, who was fixing him with one of her typical indignant Lila looks. Lila Fowler was a real catch, and Bruce was amazed by the number of times he found himself reminded of that fact. From her cute, button nose—which was constantly in the air—to her fiery brown eyes, which flashed with haughty annoyance, she was a real beauty. And Lila had a sense of fun, which was why Bruce knew she'd appreciate his Sigma pledge story.

As a plate of steaming oysters was set down in front of him, Bruce continued recounting his tale of brilliance. He could remember every second of it perfectly—the blubbering and screaming of five Sigma pledges convinced they were about to get fried when all along it had been nothing more than a hysterical hazing ritual.

Bruce smiled with satisfaction. The hoax had been his idea, and all his Sigma brothers had congratulated him on his ingenuity afterward. It wasn't as if Bruce needed reassurance that he was the big man on campus at SVU, but he wasn't about to shy away from any reminders either.

"Yes, yes, more lime," Lila intoned, waving her hand impatiently as the subservient waiter hovered around her like a puppet on strings. "Bruce, don't you think these frat pranks are just the teensiest bit dangerous?" she griped, pursing her glossy lips.

"You could go to jail for that kind of thing, you know. It's, like, illegal or something."

"Dangerous? Illegal? Of course not!" Bruce scoffed. "With four of us brothers on the outside, the situation was completely under control. Although"—he paused to chuckle as he poured garlic butter onto his oysters—"there was *one* hairy moment when the closet door caught fire by mistake. But once we found a fire extinguisher that worked, we took care of that pretty quickly. Man, it was sweet! I crack myself up just thinking about it!"

"Hmmmph!" Lila tossed her hair. "I'm cracking up just hearing about it," she replied frostily.

Bruce smiled, a faraway look in his eye. Life was just too cool right now. He had everything he needed: a babe with an attitude, a never-ending cash flow, and good buddies at Sigma house. Sighing with pleasure, Bruce drenched an oyster in sauce and popped it into his mouth. Did he have *the* life or what?

"Honestly, sometimes Lila is dimmer than a five-watt bulb," Jessica complained as Elizabeth locked the door to their dorm room behind them. "I mean, there we were, standing in front of the reigning Princess of Prissdom, who was, as usual, looking down her nose at us, and when I suggest the library, Lila looks at me like I'd just told her I was taking tango lessons with the Unabomber. . . ."

As Jessica chattered on, Elizabeth went into auto-receive mode—a habit she'd fallen back on almost all her life. Tuning out her twin sister's voice until it became white noise was a necessary coping mechanism for anyone who spent a lot of time with her. But today Elizabeth actually wished she *could* focus on Jessica's babbling. She just couldn't stop her mind from wandering into bad neighborhoods. All afternoon she'd been feeling really strange—jittery and tense and completely unlike her usual relaxed self.

It's just the weather, Elizabeth told herself for the nth time that day. Somehow the thought failed to comfort her.

"Hey, check it out!" Jessica murmured as they stepped onto the quad. "Cooool."

Elizabeth's eyes followed Jessica's gaze upward to the sky and a little shiver ran through her body, like a small electrical pulse. The evening sky was now a deep, navy-violet and the thick clouds had gathered in a weird, ringlike formation, encircling the quad perfectly. The scene was as beautiful as it was sinister, but Elizabeth couldn't shake off the forbidding vibes. It was as if the sky, with its strange cloud pattern, was sending her a message.

"Welcome to the twilight zone," Jessica muttered. Her look of amazement had turned to one of grave concern.

Good, Elizabeth thought. At least she wasn't the only one who was spooked.

As they made their way into the quad, Elizabeth took deep breaths to relax herself. Nothing was really wrong. As if the sky could send scary messages to her personally! Elizabeth almost chuckled out loud at the thought. As she smiled at several familiar faces, she knew she was totally safe. So a few freaky clouds were hovering above campus. *So what?*

Elizabeth rounded the corner of the quad, feeling lighter with every step. She even began to feel better about Tom. Anyone who spent so much time looking for flaws in their relationship would inevitably come up disappointed. It was just a question of attitude. And it was about time she changed hers—starting immediately.

Out of the corner of her eye Elizabeth caught someone smiling at her from afar. As the tall figure approached, she froze, all her good feelings dying.

Elizabeth closed her eyes deliberately and shook her head. *Stop!* she commanded herself. Slowly she opened her eyes, but nothing had changed. The vision that greeted her was exactly the same and moving toward her in slow motion. A handsome, smiling face, full lips, thick hair, and eyes as cold as chips of ice from a Norwegian glacier.

There could be no mistaking William White.

What's the use of dressing up? Lila fumed. She glanced down at her brand-new black-and-gold sweater dress made exclusively for her by a top couturier in Italy. Why look ultraglamorous for Bruce if he barely even noticed her?

Lila clenched her dessert spoon in her right hand and stared down into her crème brûlée helplessly. She didn't feel like eating a single morsel of the delectable sweet, her favorite. At that moment she'd have preferred to sink into it.

Everything Lila had told Jessica that day had returned just to slap her in the face. If only she could take back everything she had said about Bruce being the perfect man. She had spoken *waaay* too soon.

First of all, he had been late for dinner because he'd finished his workout late. Another evening maybe Lila wouldn't have been quite so annoyed, but this was a special occasion. They were celebrating the second time they'd ever had dinner together—an incredibly romantic event. Not that Bruce appeared to think so. He hadn't even mentioned the undeniable specialness of the occasion and in fact appeared to have forgotten the significance of the date altogether. No gift, no nothing.

It wasn't as if she had expected much either. A big anniversary demanded something that would really take her breath away, but for this particular occasion a small token of love would have sufficed—a pair of two-carat diamond studs in her champagne, perhaps, or simply a few Hermés silk scarves.

Not exactly a stretch, Lila thought in anger as

Bruce kept ranting about the stupid pranks he'd pulled on his Sigma pledges. At the very least he'd be paying for dinner, although it was hardly a comfort, considering her crushing disappointment.

You'd better shape up, Bruce, Lila thought as her spoon cracked the sugared glaze of her crème brûlée, sending a shard of caramel into the air. *Take that!* she thought happily as the caramel arced through the air and landed in Bruce's hair.

But Bruce didn't even notice. "I just can't get the sound of those screaming pledges out of my head!" he boomed.

"Apparently not." Lila's voice was as sharp and cold as icicles, but it could have been the melted sugar in Bruce's hair for all the effect it had. Bored, Lila glanced at her sapphire-studded watch, a gift from Bruce . . . back when he used to appreciate her.

Lila stroked the elegant gold links of the watch and sighed. Bruce had presented it to her only a week ago. It felt like a lifetime.

"Your check," the waiter intoned, breaking into Lila's sad train of thought.

Good! Lila brightened. Since the evening had been so tedious, at least the whole night wasn't lost. They still had time to check out the CyberDreams event. Then maybe she could put this whole nasty nonevent of dinner behind her.

"Hey, Li, can you get this?" Bruce asked, casually sliding the bill in Lila's direction. "Sorry," he added with a yawn. "I was so busy rushing from the gym that I forgot to go pick up my wallet."

"Forgot. To pick up. Your wallet." Lila dropped each word as if it were a block of lead.

"Yeah. I didn't take it to the gym, and I didn't have time to pick it up." Bruce shrugged, oblivious to the tone of Lila's voice. "You know, if *you* went to the gym every once in a while . . ."

Fuming, Lila picked up the check, holding it between two of her long nails as if it were a dead rat. *Perfect man, my inheritance!* she thought in angry silence as she skimmed her Gold MasterCard across the table. Paying for dinner was no problem, of course. In theory. But Lila was not pleased.

This had better be the last time, Bruce. She glared coldly at him from across the table. *After tonight, you're on probation.*

Someone help me! Elizabeth begged silently, too much in shock to open her mouth and scream. All she could do was watch helplessly as William White bore down on her, step by painstaking step. Terror catapulted her heart into her throat.

Yet there was nothing she could do but watch, rooted to the spot, as William filled her field of vision. He strode toward her, a broad, terrifying grin stretched tightly across his face. His mouth twisted into an evil smile of recognition. His cold eyes tracked hers like a hunter advancing on his prey. His . . .

Elizabeth blinked. *His?* She frowned in confusion. *His? Whose?* Blinking again, Elizabeth felt her heart slow to a gentle thud as the man before her came into focus. It wasn't William at all. It wasn't even someone who bore the faintest resemblance to William. It was simply an anonymous guy in a good mood. And already he'd passed her by.

Questions clanged inside Elizabeth's head. She felt giddy with a mixture of relief and confusion.

"Liz! You look like you just saw a ghost!" Jessica's voice jolted her back to reality.

"I thought I did," Elizabeth mumbled. "But it was nothing." Nothing but the strange purple light playing tricks on her eyes, she reasoned.

Nothing . . . nothing . . .

The word echoed through Elizabeth's mind, and after a minute she felt better. Almost totally herself again. Almost, but not quite. No matter how much she tried to blame the weather for her strange state of mind, Elizabeth couldn't fully shake the feeling that something was, in fact, very wrong. She could feel it, an instinctive knowledge welling up from deep within.

If that wasn't William, then why were you so frightened? whispered her inner voice.

Elizabeth couldn't answer that question.

"Whoa, Liz! Hold it!" Jessica turned on her heel so that she faced Elizabeth and stopped her from walking by placing two hands firmly on her shoulders. "What's the deal? Spill!"

"Huh? What do you mean?"

Elizabeth's voice was small and faraway and something else . . . frightened? And it wasn't just her voice. It was everything about her. She'd been acting weird all afternoon—like a puppy on the Fourth of July. Not her usual bossy, no-nonsense self.

"Nothing's wrong," Elizabeth insisted, her eyes skittering from left to right.

"Yeah, and I'm donating my weekends to the Salvation Army."

"Not a bad idea," Elizabeth joked weakly, averting her eyes. Jessica folded her arms and fixed Elizabeth with a stern look. "Don't try to get me off the subject," she warned. "I know you better than anyone else, Ms. Wakefield, and I can see when things are not A-OK in Lizland. Now, are you going to tell me what's up, or will we have to stand here all night?"

"I'm fine," Elizabeth replied. "Honestly. I just thought I saw someone . . . but I didn't. That's it."

"Hmmm . . ." Jessica wasn't quite buying it. But then again, when Elizabeth had something to hide, there was no way she'd talk. Jessica shook her head, half annoyed and half impressed by her twin's stubbornness. "Well, Liz, I can see you've taken a vow of silence on whatever it is, so I won't bother trying to draw blood from the proverbial stone."

"Jess . . ." Elizabeth trailed off. Jessica knew

she was on to something and Elizabeth knew *she* knew, but whatever it was, Elizabeth wouldn't budge.

"I only hope it's nothing serious," Jessica began, "because . . . you know . . . it really, really hurts my feelings when you won't confide in me!" she whined, ready to turn on the waterworks if necessary. "It makes me feel so . . . unworthy. Like you can't trust me with your secrets. That is just *so* unfair!" Jessica pouted and toed the ground like a second grader. If anything worked with Elizabeth, it was pushing the guilt button. But Elizabeth's lips remained zippered.

Fine! Jessica thought in irritation, growing bored. Whatever it was, it obviously wasn't important and could wait until after the more pressing matter of scoping out guys at the CyberDreams tent. But apparently Elizabeth wasn't up for it.

"I should get some homework done," she volunteered feebly as an excuse.

"Homework!" Jessica rolled her eyes. "Liz, for once can you stifle the urge to nerd out on a Friday? After all, it's not every weekend that this CyberDreams deal comes to SVU!"

"I'm surprised *you* want to go," Elizabeth replied with a small smile. "I never pegged you for the virtual reality type."

"There are a lot of things about me you don't know. As a matter of fact, I think this whole cyberthing is fascinating—," Jessica continued airily.

"Oh, I get it," Elizabeth interjected just as Jessica was beginning to explain what she liked about computers. "Of course! Every guy on campus will be out tonight."

Jessica sniffed in annoyance. "There's more to life than guys," she retorted, but even to her the response sounded weak. The truth was, as usual Elizabeth had read her like a book. Computers were only as fun as the guys playing with them. "OK!" she trilled, holding her hands out in defeat. "You got me. I want to check out the talent, not the technology. So sue me!"

"Thought so!" Elizabeth chuckled knowingly. "But you don't need me. Scoping is something you can do all by yourself. And anyway, I think virtual reality and all related cybergames are a total waste of time and energy."

"But that's the definition of fun, Liz! Wasting time! Not everything in life has to end in moral, cultural, or educational gratification, you know. And I *do* need you!" Jessica wheedled. "Pleeease?"

"Aren't you going with Lila?"

Jessica made a face. "Yeah, like she'll be any fun. Lila will just talk about her el perfecto boyfriend all night—that is, if they aren't fused at the lips." Jessica sighed theatrically. "Being around them is positively disgusting."

"Yeah, well, I can't stop Bruce and Lila's love fest, Jess."

"It would just be so nice to have a little sisterly

support. So I don't feel lonely," Jessica added forlornly.

Elizabeth looked torn. "We-ell . . ."

"Come on, Liz." Jessica widened her eyes to complete her best pleading expression. "You know you want to help me. I can't squelch my boredom without you."

"OK," Elizabeth agreed with a laugh.

"Great!" Jessica cheered, feeling the familiar thrill of victory. She might not always be able to read Elizabeth like a book, but she sure could play her like a harp.

Chapter Three

"Aargh!" Tom hurled his calculus book at the wall. "Enough!" he bellowed, standing up from his desk. It was a Friday night, after all, and despite what he'd suggested to Elizabeth earlier that day, homework could wait.

Yawning, Tom crossed the room. He felt lazy, and his comfortable bed seemed to be beckoning to him. Tom kicked off his sneakers and flopped onto his bed all in one deft move. Smiling, he glanced at the framed photo on his nightstand. Elizabeth smiled back at him.

Tom lifted the frame and studied it close-up. It was a shot he loved—Elizabeth lying in a field of cornflowers as blue as her eyes. *I'm a lucky man!* Tom thought with satisfaction. He curled his hands lazily behind his head and settled comfortably into his pillow, staring at the ceiling and basking in the pleasure of feeling so good.

If he'd been outside, he'd have counted his lucky stars. Tom just couldn't believe how well things were going between him and Elizabeth. In the past they'd seen their share of ups and downs, but now everything was stable and secure. They had finally reached the point where they were totally comfortable and knew each other backward and forward.

No more misunderstandings, Tom thought with relief. So many times he and Elizabeth had almost lost each other because of some miscommunication, but that could never happen now. They were so in tune, they could practically read each other's minds. He was willing to bet she was walking into Reid Hall right at that moment, dashing up to his door to ask him out for a late coffee or a movie-slash-make-out sesh in the Dickenson Hall TV lounge.

Bingo! Tom leaped to his feet and grinned. The knock on his bedroom door came right on cue. "Just a sec," he called as he ran his hands through his dark brown hair. After a check down south to make sure he was wearing something more substantial than boxers, he reached for the door handle.

"Hey!" Elizabeth smiled and kissed Tom on the cheek. "I see you're working hard," she added in a teasing voice, inclining her head at the math book that Tom had thrown at the wall.

"Too hard," Tom replied. "If I see another cosine curve, my head will explode."

"So Friday-night studying is out, I take it?"

"Way out. Some serious vegging is in order, I think. You were right—this is a good weekend for videos." Tom enfolded Elizabeth in a bear hug and kissed the top of her head. A cozy night watching videos together or playing cards was exactly what Tom felt like. Nothing special—just the two of them alone together.

"I have another suggestion."

"What's that, hon?"

"The Virtual Reality Fair."

"You mean that CyberDreams thing?" Tom stepped out of Elizabeth's embrace and gave her a searching look to see if she was kidding. Virtual reality and Elizabeth didn't exactly go together.

She looked perfectly serious. "It could be fun," she insisted, completely straight-faced.

"I don't know. . . ." Tom scratched his head in amazement. Since when would Elizabeth pass up a low-key evening with him for some dumb computer fair with every idiot on campus? Something weird was up.

"I think we should give it a go," she added. "Beats hanging around doing noth—"

"Well, if that's what you want." Tom shrugged. "But I'd rather stay in with you."

"Let's just go for one hour. Then you'll have me all to yourself."

This was too weird. Virtual reality was so . . . *un*-Elizabeth, and yet here she was practically *bargaining* with Tom to go. "All right," Tom replied grudgingly.

"Great! Meet me at my room in half an hour? OK!" she said without even waiting for a response. Before Tom knew it, she was out the door.

"See you then." Tom closed the door behind Elizabeth and flopped back onto his bed. He couldn't deny the disappointment that welled up inside him. Going out in this freaky, unpleasant weather was the last thing he felt like doing. And to dork around in virtual reality? It made no sense whatsoever. Oh, well, too bad for Tom. Chalk up another one for the Lizmeister.

Maybe it will be fun, Tom told himself, but he wasn't exactly convinced. Nor was he still convinced that he and Elizabeth were on the same wavelength.

Well, so much for being in tune. And so much for the quiet evening with the girlfriend he *thought* he knew.

"Can they open those doors already? It's after eight!" Jessica tapped her foot impatiently, her eyes fixed on the entrance to the CyberDreams tent. Waiting was one thing she simply could *not* tolerate, especially when it involved being jostled by a small crowd of sweaty, hyperkeen computer geeks.

Not exactly a great turnout, she thought in annoyance, rolling her eyes as an overconfident nerd tried to smile at her. *Know your place!* she wanted to shout at him. Jessica was practically shooting staples out of her eyes as she stared him down. Finally the geek shrank back into the crowd, filling Jessica with welcome relief. She hated dealing with guys who dared to graze too high up in the food chain.

"Move over, Jess! You're about to step on my new mules." Lila looked just as irritated as Jessica felt, although why, Jessica couldn't tell. Bruce was there, trailing Lila like a faithful puppy. And although her pale suede mules were indeed in danger of being scuffed, that hardly gave her grounds for moodiness.

"Why does everyone have to push?" Elizabeth demanded crossly, trying to make space for Tom to slide into the line next to her. "This isn't the front row at a Beastie Boys concert or anything."

Another moody one, Jessica thought, her irritation escalating. Lila, Elizabeth, even Tom—they were all bugging Jessica with their petty behavior. And being around these walking dishcloths was seriously jeopardizing Jessica's own state of mind. Then, as if that weren't enough, Jessica had had the unfortunate experience of making eye contact with Alison Quinn twice in the last half hour. One polite wave she could manage, but two was pushing it.

Perhaps this cybersoiree was a bad idea after all, Jessica thought, miffed at making a huge waste of her precious Friday-night time. But just as she was about to turn on her heel and stalk back to

Dickenson, she spotted two potential hotties at the same time. One was blond and deeply tanned; the other was more rough around the edges, with a stubbly beard and messy, shoulder-length curls. Both acknowledged her with a nod, and Jessica smiled back demurely. They weren't exactly alpha males, but they were enough to keep her in line—literally. In Jessica's experience a few "maybes" often promised a "definite," and she was perfectly content to stick around a while longer for the "definite" stud to emerge.

"At last, a sign of life!" Lila murmured as the tent door rippled, then flapped open.

Jessica craned her neck to get a better look and . . .

Whoa!

Just as she turned her attention to the tent flap, out stepped a tall, lanky, drop-dead gorgeous guy, as if in answer to Jessica's prayers. Wearing loose-fitting black pants and a black, short-sleeve dress shirt, he looked both suave and scraggly at the same time.

Mmmm. Just my type, Jessica thought, admiring the pantherlike way the stranger moved to a podium set up in front of the tent. After a moment he looked up. Jessica felt her breath catch in her throat. His short, slightly punky black hair was cool enough, but his almost sinister, dark eyebrows were the key. Dark and well shaped, they truly made him sexy. Not to mention that lazy look of slight superiority he wore. He was sleek and kind of . . . enigmatic. *Perfecto!*

"Ladies and gentlemen, your attention, please!"

"I can give you that," Jessica purred. Lila giggled, nudging Jessica with her elbow.

"My name is Jonah Falk, and I'm here to introduce you to the best, the wildest, and definitely the weirdest adventure of your lives. . . ." He paused and gave the crowd a cool once-over. "If you're willing, that is."

"Oh, I'm willing . . . and able," Jessica murmured, transfixed.

"CyberDreams welcomes you to the experience of a lifetime," Jonah continued as Jessica looked on in openmouthed adoration. "And let me assure you, once you enter this tent, you will not be disappointed."

I certainly hope not, Jessica thought dreamily as she gazed into Jonah's glittering, coal black eyes. Divinely mysterious.

"Now, if you'll give me a moment," Jonah added, "I'll tell you everything you need to know. . . ."

Jessica's heartbeat accelerated and a familiar warmth began to spread through her chest as Jonah began his explanation of CyberDreams, speaking in harsh, gravelly tones that seemed to graze their fingernails right over Jessica's skin.

Now this is a man, Jessica mused, watching Jonah but barely hearing a word of his speech. CyberWhat?

CyberWho? She couldn't care any less about experiencing CyberAnything, let alone CyberDreams. *Her* dream was standing right there. In the flesh.

"What we have here is possibly the most advanced cybertechnology that the world has to offer. . . ."

I'll believe that *when I see it!* Bruce scoffed silently. Still, he had to admit he was intrigued. This Jonah dude looked pretty confident up on his podium, and the huge white tent against the freaky purple sky made quite an impression. Bruce figured the guy must have been hiding some powerful purple smoke machines someplace. No way could the sky turn that color for real.

"Some of you probably don't believe me," Jonah added, scanning the crowd as if sensing Bruce's skepticism. "And if you don't, then *I* won't bother trying to convince you. Just come on in and see for yourself. This"—he paused and dropped his voice—"is the rush you've been waiting for."

"Aww yeah!" Bruce bellowed the second he heard the word *rush.* He bobbed his head in anticipation. Thrill seeking was definitely what Bruce Patman was all about, and if this CyberDream thing provided a rush of *any* kind, Bruce wanted in—and pronto.

"What we have here"—Jonah indicated vaguely

the compound behind him—"is the latest in cybertechnological advancement. To put it in layman's terms, we have state-of-the-art machines specifically designed to give you exactly what you need for the CyberDream of your life."

Bruce's ears perked up even more. This was sounding better and better! Sure, Bruce didn't have a clue what the guy was talking about, but he was willing to accept just about anything as long as it was state-of-the-art and specifically designed to give him exactly what he needed. It was a tall order to fill, but at only a few bucks a pop this sounded like a pretty fair gamble.

"The principle behind CyberDreams is that our machines will pull your deepest fantasies—your wildest dreams—from your subconscious and then present them to you as reality in an adventure perfectly tailored to fit you and only you."

Jonah paused as the crowd began to murmur excitedly. Bruce felt Lila clutch his arm. He squeezed his bicep in response. Man, this was going to rock! Adrenaline already pumped through Bruce's body as he imagined himself pulling some macho, daredevil stunt in cyberspace. He couldn't quite picture it, but he knew it involved helicopters, the Grand Canyon, and lots of explosives.

"There are only a few rules about CyberDreams," Jonah intoned. "Number one: No one can dream more than once a day. Number two: No one can dream more than twice ever, or else you risk permanent damage to your sensory system. But don't worry," Jonah added as a nervous ripple went through the crowd, "if you stick to the rules, you can't go wrong and absolutely no damage can be done. Guaranteed."

"You can count me in," Bruce murmured, his pulse racing. He couldn't quite absorb what Jonah had just talked about—something about dreams being dangerous. Well, everyone knew that danger was Bruce Patman's drug of choice. His only worry was that the CyberDreams wouldn't even *compare* to his pulse pounding everyday life.

"I welcome you once again to the ultimate virtual reality experience," Jonah continued, stepping back from the open tent door. "Welcome once again to CyberDreams. Where your dreams become reality. Where your reality is still . . . just a dream."

"Yeah, yeah," Bruce muttered. He lunged forward with the crowd, unable to contain his excitement any longer. Dreams, reality, whatever. If it gave Bruce a buzz, he'd give up his cash.

Permanent damage . . .

Jonah's words echoed in Elizabeth's mind. She didn't like the sound of that at all.

Although, she reminded herself, *he did* guarantee *that CyberDreams couldn't harm you if you followed the rules.*

Still, there was something a little off-color about the very idea of CyberDreams. Elizabeth wasn't sure that messing with people's minds was quite as harmless as Jonah made it out to be. After all, who knew what lurked in someone's subconscious? Maybe bringing it to the surface wasn't such a great idea.

"So what do you think?" Elizabeth asked Tom.

"I don't know." Tom's tone was flat, disinterested.

"We don't have to go in, you know," Elizabeth replied, half annoyed at Tom's attitude and half relieved. If he wasn't up for it, then at least Elizabeth could use him as an excuse to leave.

"It's up to you." Tom shrugged noncommittally.

Elizabeth sighed. Why was Tom insisting on being so dull? He never used to be that way. The Tom she used to know always had strong opinions, always knew what he wanted and wasn't afraid to say it out loud. He'd always been a leader, not a follower.

"It's not just up to me," Elizabeth replied testily, folding her arms. "If you don't want to go, then just say so."

"Jeez, Liz. You don't have to get so snippy." Elizabeth stiffened at the edge in Tom's voice. "It's not a big deal—it's just a stupid gimmick, that's all."

Elizabeth immediately felt her face redden. Tom was right. This wasn't worth getting in a lather over.

"I'm sorry," she said. "I guess . . . I'm just a little tense today. Wanna bag it?" she added, jerking her head at the tent.

"Well . . ." Tom smiled. "As long as I'm here, I might as well give it a try. Although," he added, putting his arm lightly around Elizabeth's shoulders, "I'd still rather be away from this crowd."

But at least we're out doing *something for a change,* Elizabeth found herself thinking. Whether CyberDreams was dumb or not, it certainly beat sitting around in Tom's room or at Dickenson, talking about the weather.

Whoa! Negativity alert! Elizabeth bit her lip as they shuffled forward in the line. Tom was making an effort . . . for once. Why couldn't she just be happy with that? As hard as she tried, she just couldn't *feel* happy, that's why. No matter how hard she tried to force herself to relax, her shoulders felt as stiff as cast-iron beams. No matter how hard she tried to force herself into a more positive frame of mind, she couldn't shake her general feeling of worry and unease. Part of it was Tom and the problems they were having, but there was something else too.

Maybe it was the weird weather. Maybe it was the slightly creepy aura Jonah Falk had about him. Elizabeth wasn't sure. But either way, she wasn't thrilled about placing her precious brain in the hands of this mystery man and his mystery employers.

Nervously Elizabeth glanced at the white tent, looming closer now, like a giant . . .

. . . tombstone.

Elizabeth jumped, her heart pattering like the wings of a frightened bird. What put that morbid image into her head? She blinked at the tent and gave it a good, hard, grim stare. It didn't look anything like a tombstone. It looked exactly like . . . a big white tent. What a shocker! Tombstones, William White . . . she needed to stop imagining things.

But even that seemed somehow impossible. She couldn't put her feelings into words, but something was going down on the SVU campus—something sinister. She couldn't be sure exactly what the threat was or where it was coming from. As she forced her legs to move in the direction of the CyberDreams tent, Elizabeth couldn't ignore the slight tremor that danced through her body at the thought of what unimaginable fears lay behind the blank white sheets.

Boooooom!

Elizabeth jumped. Another lightning bolt had snaked down from the sky like a giant silver lizard, illuminating the white rosebud on the front of the tent. Elizabeth stood still for a second, paralyzed by a bolt of fear so sharp, she could actually taste it, metallic on her tongue. Was it her imagination, or did the rosebud seem to . . . open?

Just as quickly as the thought came, it disappeared, overshadowed by Elizabeth's practical inner voice. *Just get over yourself already,* the voice snapped. *You're a journalist, not a Psychic Friend. Remember?*

Elizabeth gulped and lifted her chin with determination. Hallucinating that embroidered rosebuds were opening before her eyes—now, *that* was ridiculous. The unwelcome memory of William White had simply dredged up some residual fear inside her—not to mention plenty of irrational thoughts.

You're going to go into that tent and have a blast, Elizabeth ordered herself, taking Tom's arm and marching forward. When they neared the entrance, Elizabeth got out her wallet to pay admission, a smile on her face. Everything but fun, happy thoughts had been banished from her mind. After all, if the CyberDreams pitchman was to be believed, it was her fantasies, not her fears, that were about to be tapped by the dream machines.

But just as Elizabeth slid a five-dollar bill from her wallet, she couldn't help but let her eyes slide up to the white rosebud on the billowing banner above her head. She didn't want to, but she simply couldn't control her eyes. Thankfully, the rosebud didn't appear to be opening. But still, it seemed almost to be staring at Elizabeth . . . *calling to her.*

Instinctively Elizabeth shrank back and placed a hand on her palpitating heart as if she could slow it down. She tried to breathe deeply, but it did nothing to calm her.

And then she saw them in her mind's eye again—millions and millions of white roses multiplying into a pattern, into infinity. . . .

No! Elizabeth closed her eyes and reopened them. Her perpetually overworked mind was simply playing tricks on her, she knew. But she couldn't shake the feeling that somehow, defying all laws of logic and reality, *he* was there. She could feel it in her bones and in her blood. With each beat of her pulse Elizabeth could feel him. It was as if William White had climbed up out of his grave and was tracking his ghostly footprints across her heart.

Chapter Four

"Geek alert!" Lila moaned as a spindly, overexcited kid with pasty skin lurched in front of her toward the tent door. "*Must* we circulate with these plebs?" she wailed.

"If you want to experience your greatest fantasy, you have to endure the dweeb brigade," Jessica replied.

"This better be worth it," Lila complained. "Because so far, this experience is hardly living up to my greatest fantasy. More like a giant waste of time." She stifled a gag as another guy, dressed from head to toe in *Star Trek* gear, pushed past her.

"It'll be great, Li, I promise you," Jessica replied. "Just think—your fantasy adventure is only minutes away." *And so is mine,* Jessica thought with a sigh, her eyes locked tight onto Jonah Falk's bod. She could only see him in profile since the nerds had him pretty much surrounded, but even this half view was enough to keep her going. She nearly melted as her eyes lingered on Jonah's strong chin. *Let the nerds have him now,* she thought indulgently. *He'll belong to me soon enough.*

"Fantasy adventure!" Lila snorted in derision. "Right now I'd settle for a long soak in the tub."

"In your CyberDream you can have anything you want, Lila. Picture it—your wildest dream come true!"

"My wildest dream. But haven't I lived it already?"

"Anything's possible in virtual reality," Jessica replied. "That's the beauty of it."

"We'll see about that, Geek of the Week," Lila retorted. But somehow she looked a little more optimistic. "If I could have anything in the world . . . ," she murmured, furrowing her brow in concentration. "Money is no object. Only the limits of my imagination. Hmmm . . ."

Within seconds Lila's eyes misted over. No doubt she was imagining bathing in diamonds and showering in pearls. Who knew what freaky things lay in the deepest recesses of Lila Fowler's imagination? Jessica didn't even want to go there. But at least she was able to shut the diva up for a while.

Still, Jessica couldn't help wondering if Lila really *had* lived her wildest dream already. Lila's fantasy universe would probably involve tons and tons of baubles and other luxury items, as well as hours and hours of admiring herself in front of endless mirrors . . . yawn! That was Lila's everyday life, all right. But Jessica's fantasy could just as well be as realistic as Lila's. Having Jonah all to herself in real life wasn't exactly a stretch. As soon as he saw her, Jessica was confident the electricity would be mutual.

Either way I'm about to find out! Jessica thought as a crowd of people pushed into the tent, leaving her standing only a few feet away from Jonah. Before he had a chance to see her, Jessica quickly gave her hair an expert flip and fluffed it with her fingertips. Standing in line was such a bad-hair-inducing activity.

Jonah turned to face her. Jessica put on her sultriest look: a sexy smile and raised eyebrows. She wanted Jonah to see that she approved of his hotness—hence the smile. But at the same time the arched eyebrows would give off an aloof, mysterious air . . . just like his did.

It worked. Jonah gazed at her full on, his coal black eyes toying with hers.

Hel-lo!

Jonah was even foxier up close. His skin was smooth and tanned, his hair gleaming.

One second . . . two seconds . . . now look away!

As she tossed her hair and averted her eyes casually, Jessica wanted to give herself a standing O for not coming on too strong. Flirting was a fine art, and she prided herself on knowing the rules inside out. This particular situation called for the dine-and-dash. Step one: She let the flirt object know she was interested by feasting upon him with her eyes. Step two: The moment she sensed the flirt object's ego puffing up, she gave him a run for his money.

It's working! Jessica thought with a smug little smile. She could practically feel Jonah's piercing gaze prickling the side of her casually turned cheek. *Girl, you are* too *good!*

"Do you think having those dorky *Star Trek* types in the same tent will lower the glamour level of my dream?" Lila asked, her voice interrupting Jessica's love connection like call waiting.

Jessica sighed in annoyance. Trust Lila to bust what, quite possibly, could have turned out to be one of the most important grooves of her entire life.

"Lower the glamour level? What, are you *kidding*? Of *course* not!" Jessica snapped, her hopes spiraling downward as Jonah turned away and began talking to another freshwoman. "CyberDreams are *personalized!*" she went on. "Didn't you hear the speech? Each dream is tailored to the dreamer. You should try listening once in a while, Li. You might just learn something."

"Jeez!" Lila huffed. "I was only checking. Bad fashion is contagious, you know, and these techie twits have a serious color-coordinating disorder."

"I know. Sorry, Li." Jessica forced her tone

down from carcinogenic to conciliatory since Jonah's eyes were once again trained on her own. As a matter of fact, they were now only inches away. "One ticket, please." She lowered her eyelashes demurely.

"Coming right up." Jonah smiled lazily and handed Jessica her change. "Enjoy your fantasy."

"Believe me, I will."

Here goes.

Elizabeth swallowed nervously as she stepped through the tent door. Her stomach was still in knots, but she willed herself to move forward. There was nowhere else to go. Running back to her dorm room would only cause Tom unnecessary anxiety. And anyway, being alone in Dickenson wouldn't exactly be a comfort. The day had been bad enough—there was no sense in making it worse. Still, the thought of some cybergadget messing with her already messy mind didn't do much to calm her.

But what choice do I have? Elizabeth thought with a sigh. She'd already paid. The only way out was in.

Elizabeth glanced nervously around her. The decor seemed innocuous enough. Inside the compound was a small main room surrounded by ten cubicles that had been partitioned off from one another by white sheets. She'd somehow expected something more sinister looking. But although the space was bigger inside than it seemed from outside, there was nothing else in any way surprising or forbidding. Nothing more than a bunch of little rooms made from sheets.

Big deal, Elizabeth thought with relief as she walked to booth number three—the number designated on her ticket.

The inside of Elizabeth's cubicle was equally unthreatening. Just a headset with goggles and a chair facing a large screen. Not a creepy white rosebud in sight. Still, Elizabeth was on her guard. She sat down gingerly and toyed with her headset for a moment before putting it on.

As she settled into her seat, she began to feel a familiar sensation . . . a journalist's curiosity. Elizabeth embraced it. High time she started feeling like herself again!

She slid the supplied earphones onto her ears and adjusted the visual apparatus to fit her head. The moment had come to push all unpleasant thoughts away and find out exactly what CyberDreams were all about.

A few seconds passed. The goggles were dark, and Elizabeth heard nothing. Then a buzz of static, crisp and loud, filled her earphones.

Quickly a tremor of anticipation arced up Elizabeth's spine. She hunched forward, waiting for something to happen.

My greatest adventure. My wildest dream . . .

She tried to guess what the machines could pull

up from her deepest, innermost self. Who knew? It might actually turn out to be fun. Now *that* would be a shocker!

"Oh, my . . . ," Lila breathed in reverence as her eyes adjusted to the scene before her. Nothing could have prepared her for the gorgeous vision that lay beyond the hologrammed door of her CyberDreams screen. She had stepped into a vast emporium, bigger than any shopping mall, with rows and rows of giant skylights illuminating rack upon rack of clothing. Transfixed, her lips slightly parted in wonder, Lila began her slow descent into the room by way of a crystal staircase made by none other than Mr. Baccarat himself, as the gleaming inscription on the balustrade informed her.

Her footsteps echoing on the glinting stairs, Lila paused, suddenly overcome. The beauty of the room, flooded with light, was almost more than she could bear. *It's like a church,* she thought, moved almost to the point of tears. So many coat hangers, all dripping with rainbow colors belonging to hundreds of gowns and shoes and hats and scarves . . . The sight of so much good taste all at once called for a moment of genuflection. Lila bowed her head in respectful awe, remaining still for a moment—just a moment, however, and the moment soon passed. It was time to get moving. It was time to shop.

"This is unbelievable!" Lila shrieked, her voice

reverberating through the huge, hangarlike boutique. Couture gowns in rich jewel tones beckoned to her from between shimmering jackets and wraps spun from a gossamer lighter than butterfly wings. And each one hung from a solid gold coat hanger.

"Jean-Yves duPres!" Lila cheered in delight, whipping a scarlet satin pantsuit from its hanger and examining its label. "And a Cristiano Belladonna original," she murmured, her fingers tracing the skirt of a hand-embroidered olive green ball gown. Closer inspection of other garments revealed what Lila had only dared to hope for. *All* of her favorite designers were here, under the very same roof. And what was more, every single item Lila had seen—every exquisitely chic bias-cut dress and flamboyantly original handmade shoe—was exactly Lila's size.

"My size!" Lila crowed in delight, picking up yet another must-have little black number. "My size again!" She snatched a pale blue suede jacket. If ever there was a sign from above that said "you must shop," this had to be it!

But what to choose? This part Lila hated. Even *she* knew she couldn't have *everything* in the whole store. Even *she* realized that would be excessive. She would just have to settle for ten or thirty new outfits. She couldn't be greedy. But she couldn't help pouting as she returned an adorable silver sheath to its hanger.

"Don't put it back," a voice whispered from behind. "It was *made* for you."

As Lila spun around, she saw a suave, dark-haired man loitering behind a rack of beaded cashmere sweaters. A tasteful, clearly expensive dark suit hung off broad shoulders, and his smoldering gaze sizzled as it lingered on Lila's body. "You're perfect," he uttered, his Rolex glinting in the light.

Bruce! Pirouetting on her heel, Lila spun herself into Bruce's strong arms and gazed into his burning eyes. She rested her head on his shoulder. Her savior had arrived!

"Go on," Bruce added, gesturing at the racks groaning with spectacular designer creations. "Try them on. All of them."

"But I can't choose!" Lila whimpered.

"You don't have to," Bruce replied, a small smile playing at the corners of his mouth. "You can have anything you want. Anything. And everything."

"This?" Lila breathed, holding out her arms. "All of it . . . for me?" She widened her eyes in astonishment.

"Everything. For you, nothing but the very best."

"Whoo-hoo!" Lila spun around and around until she was giddy from the sight of all the sparkling, twinkling fabrics whirling past her eyes. She felt like Alice in Wonderland . . . or Cinderella, only with better accessories.

"Can I help you, miss?" a voice inquired humbly. A sales assistant—impeccably dressed, appearing as if from nowhere.

As Lila directed the elegant yet obsequious sales assistant, the assistant moved at the speed of light, bringing stacks and stacks of dresses, silk jackets, luxurious scarves, and diamond-studded handbags to a velvet-curtained dressing room. Then Lila initiated the fashion show of her life, parading one ensemble after another in front of Bruce's appreciative gaze. He stood dead still, riveted by Lila's extraordinary beauty, and gave only the briefest of curt nods to the assistant when an outfit was to his liking.

"And that will be . . . four million dollars, please," the salesclerk trilled as she rang up the last item and ordered several lower-class peons to begin packing the crates.

"Four *million?*" Lila gasped. "But Bruce, that's too much."

"Not at all. You deserve this, Lila." Bruce flashed his dazzling white teeth and whipped out a credit card made of solid platinum, so bright it practically blinded the clerk. "I trust this Über-Express card is acceptable?"

As the clerk stammered a reply, obviously dizzy with admiration for the rich, debonair stranger with such unbelievable purchasing power, Lila swooned and fell into Bruce's arms, batting her eyelashes in thanks.

"Darling," she whispered throatily. "You don't have to do this."

"But I must, Lila. For you, nothing is too much. . . ."

Just as Lila parted her lips for the kiss of a lifetime, an electronic beep sounded, jolting her from her dream. She blinked, but the boutique faded to static, then to a blank screen. No Bruce, no crates of haute couture, nothing.

"Tsk!" Lila tapped a long, red nail on the side of her headset, but nothing happened. Petulantly she tried again, applying more force. This prompted a reaction.

"Your CyberDream is now over," a disembodied voice announced.

"What?" Lila yelled in annoyance.

"Kindly leave the tent and remember to take all your personal belongings with you," the voice intoned coolly. "Thank you for choosing CyberDreams. Have a nice day."

"That was quick," Lila grumbled, slinging her pocketbook over her shoulder and flouncing out of the cubicle. *Far* too quick. She sighed at the thought of her lovely fashion emporium and how quickly it had vanished. *Ten measly minutes!* That wouldn't do. It wouldn't do at *all.*

Chapter Five

It's so dark in here. . . . Where am I?

Elizabeth felt panic grip her insides. Then her eyes adjusted to the dim light. She realized she was in a vast library. Stepping forward tentatively, she noticed heavy layers of dust coating the endless shelves groaning with heavy books.

It looks like no one's set foot in here for years, she thought in wonder, her shoes tracking prints in what must once have been a gleaming, polished oak floor.

Rounding a corner, Elizabeth caught her breath. Shafts of heavy, golden sunlight streaked in through frosted windows, illuminating floating dust motes and wall-to-wall steel file cabinets, hundreds upon hundreds of them, all apparently untouched. Or untouched for decades, at least . . .

What could be in them?

Her heart thumping in excitement, Elizabeth

stepped up to the largest file cabinet and gingerly traced a finger across the dusty label. "World Events/Top Secret," she read out loud. *Hmmm . . .*

Elizabeth tugged at the heavy, rusted drawer, but nothing happened. Although Elizabeth knew she was only playing a game, she couldn't help being caught up in it. Barely able to contain her rising excitement, she gripped the handle with two hands and jammed her foot against the base of the cabinet for leverage.

There!

The cabinet popped open and slid out slowly on squeaky rollers.

Now, let's see. . . .

Clapping to clear the dust from her palms, Elizabeth squinted at the rows of paper folders stacked in front of her. "World War One/Conspiracies . . . World War Two/Subterfuge and Stolen Goods," she read. And there was more. Much more. Files detailing undercover military operations in South America . . . thick envelopes claiming to contain detailed sketches of Russian nuclear submarines . . . a file on a U.S. military cover-up of an alien ship landing in Nevada in the fifties . . .

Yeah, right!

Elizabeth laughed, but she still felt the tiny hairs on her arms tickling with excitement. For a moment she lost her skepticism and allowed herself to get caught up in the experience. The cabinet was a journalist's dream, a mine of information that could change the way the world looked at history!

"Well, what are you waiting for?" Elizabeth asked herself, her hands trembling as she touched the piles of documents before her. She didn't want to hold back a moment longer, but she had no clue where to begin. Each label was so tantalizing, each file more thrilling than the next. As she skimmed her fingers down the labels, Elizabeth flipped through names and titles promising answers to long-unsolved mysteries, from the disappearance of Amelia Earhart to the truth behind the identity of Jack the Ripper. Her heart beat triple time. Which to choose?

Aha! Elizabeth's expert eye spotted a fat green file labeled simply Conspiracies: USA. Now *this* could really be something! Maybe she, Elizabeth Wakefield, would find the answers to the biggest unsolved cases of the millennium!

All of a sudden, Elizabeth froze.

Footsteps.

She'd heard footsteps.

Nothing heavy. Just a soft, steady patter. But in the huge, empty library the sound magnified and echoed off the walls in a chorus of ghostly beats. And judging by the steadily increasing sound, the footsteps were advancing in her direction.

Quickly and almost without thinking, Elizabeth ducked behind a large wooden cabinet, waiting for the mystery guest to appear.

An anxious minute passed. The footsteps died

away. Nothing was left but the sound of Elizabeth's own heartbeat rattling against her rib cage.

But where did they . . . it . . . go? she wondered. She had distinctly heard someone—or something—coming toward her. Had she imagined it?

Instinctively Elizabeth knew she hadn't. Her skin began to prickle, confirming her fears.

Someone was there.

Someone was watching her.

"Miss Wakefield, I'm going to lunch now. Oh, and your twelve o'clock is here."

Jessica nodded brusquely at her secretary. "Send him in, Moneypenny." She kicked her feet off the top of the large desk in her huge, stylishly minimal office and drained the dregs of her coffee in one smooth motion.

"Ah, Mr. Jonah . . . Falk, is it?" Jessica drummed her Montblanc pen on her desk and leaned back in her swivel chair. The devilishly handsome man entered her office, looking—despite his rakishly sexy appearance—like a nervous wreck.

Trouble. She could smell it on him. Men like him were *always* in trouble.

Jonah raked a shaking hand over the stubble on his chin. "Wakefield, I'll get to the point. My life is in serious danger. Word on the street tells me you're the best there is. Can you help me?"

"Slow down, mister," Jessica purred seductively. The guy was a mess, although he was definitely a number ten on the stud scale. She needed to calm him down. Make him . . . even easier on the eyes.

"Look." Jonah ran a hand through his thick, midnight black hair. "There's a contract on my head. I don't know who's behind this or why anyone would want to kill me, but my days are numbered. I'm in the soup, Wakefield."

"The soup, eh? Hmmm . . ." Jessica stood up and crossed the room. Walking in a microscopic black-leather miniskirt and seven-inch stilettos wasn't easy, but Jessica had it down. And regardless of how practical her outfit really wasn't, it was her signature.

Jessica Wakefield, PI, had feminine flair and an inimitable sense of style, but she wasn't the type of dame any regular Joe could push over on a dime. This Wakefield was as hard as nails and as tough as any grizzled Dick Tracy on the job. If anything, she was tougher: With a nose for sniffing out a scam and a bull's-eye way with a roscoe, Jessica Wakefield was a formidable opponent for any lowlife criminal. She was so dangerous, her own body had been state-certified as a deadly weapon. But she commanded respect and admiration for solving every case she'd ever taken—and for doing it all without ever messing up her elegant chignon.

"Now, Mr. Falk, let's take it from the top," Jessica

continued, her voice silky but cool. She sat down on the window ledge opposite Jonah and crossed her endless legs delicately, aware of his admiring gaze.

Jonah swallowed hard, reeling from the exquisite vision that filled his eyes. Jessica simply smiled knowingly. She'd seen it all too often—the effect her dazzling beauty and brilliantly capable detective's mind had on men. As a woman of substance, such reactions were par for the course.

"Well," Jonah began, his eyes flickering appreciatively over Jessica's lithe and luscious body. "I don't know what else to tell you. I'm going down and I need you."

"Yes, you do," Jessica breathed, lowering her lashes. "OK, I'll take the case. Now, don't worry. You're in *excellent* hands."

"I can see that." Jonah took a step toward Jessica as if drawn by a magnet. He reached her side and took her hand. As he raised it to his lips, Jessica closed her eyes. Jonah's mouth seared her delicate skin, the lightest brush of his lips so charged with heat, Jessica was ready to grab for the nearest fire extinguisher.

I'm melting, Jessica thought blissfully. *This is heaven, this is . . . whoa!*

Jessica stiffened at the sound of furtive footsteps outside her door. In a second her finely tuned instincts sounded a warning bell. These were not friendly visitors. This was danger, lurking only a few feet away.

Putting a finger to her scarlet lips, Jessica grabbed Jonah and hustled him out onto the window ledge. Deftly maneuvering herself atop her stilettos, she shunted Jonah ahead of her and hugged the wall until they were out of sight.

Just in time, she thought as she heard voices.

"There's no one here!" a woman complained.

"But I could have sworn I heard people talking . . . ," her male companion replied.

Jessica furrowed her brow. The voices sounded familiar, but she couldn't pin them down. The presence of this Falk fellow was somehow altering her ability to concentrate.

"Well, no sense in hanging around here," the man continued, his voice gruff. "We'd better hotfoot it over to Redhill North. If we don't bail double-quick, we'll be looking at ten."

"No way," the woman replied. "No one even knows it's missing yet. And for sure no one will think to look at the station." She laughed, a high, braying whinny. The man joined in.

Redhill North! Jessica knew the joint—a remote train-switching station on the wrong side of the tracks. Literally. Whatever those two dopes were hiding, she was going to find it first.

A ripple of adrenaline zigzagged through her body. She loved the thrill of a good mystery—or in this case, a triple mystery. Who were these people? What were they hiding? And why did they want Jonah dead?

Either way, it's all in the bag, Jessica thought confidently. *I'll nail you, suckers!*

Suddenly Jonah sneezed. Loudly.

"Hey! Did you hear that?" the woman's voice rang out.

"Let's go," Jessica whispered, grabbing Jonah's arm as he flashed her an apologetic look. "We gotta motor!"

"Where?" Jonah widened his eyes as he looked down onto the street, so far below them the cars looked like kids' toys. "We can't just jump!"

"This way." In a half second Jessica was swinging off the nearby drainpipe. In a few swift moves she pulled herself up onto the roof of the building, with Jonah following closely behind.

"They're coming after us," he yelled as Jessica pulled him to safety.

Yikes! What now? Jessica panicked as she saw a hand clamping onto the lip of the roof, followed by another hand . . . with a gun!

"We're history!" she wailed as Jonah flung himself into her arms. There was nowhere to go. They were all out of options.

"I won't let them kill us," Jonah cried. "We can't give up this easily, Wakefield!"

"*Excuse* me? Like, do *you* have any bright ideas, *Watson?*"

"Your CyberDream is now over. . . ."

Huh?

The criminal's hand froze in midmove. The

gun dissolved, then the hand, then the rooftop beneath her. Everything turned to static. Yet Jessica still stood on terra firma.

She gaped in amazement. Everything had looked and felt and sounded so real, she'd totally forgotten she was only experiencing virtual reality.

"But it can't just end there!" she complained as the screen dimmed. "Wait a minute!" Jessica shouted.

"Thank you for choosing CyberDreams. Have a nice day."

"You can't just leave me on a rooftop, for crying out loud!" she spat, banging her headset with the flat of her palm. But nothing happened.

She threw her headset to the ground and kicked it. "What a rip-off!"

OK, just calm down!

Elizabeth breathed deeply, but her heart was still jerking in her chest like a kite in a gale-force wind. She concentrated on her breathing and told herself that whoever had approached her had obviously gone away. If not, he, she, or it would have made an appearance by now. After a moment she felt better—but not much—and stood up.

Glancing fearfully to her left and right, Elizabeth saw nothing. Her heart slowed to an almost normal beat. *Don't be silly,* she berated herself, almost chuckling out loud. She knew where she was, and it wasn't a library. She was in the

CyberDreams tent, and the whole thing was only a game. A game she needed to get back to pronto—because right before her were some *very* important, highly confidential documents just begging to be read.

Of course Elizabeth knew, deep down, that no virtual library could really hold secrets to the world's greatest and most significant events. But then again, what did she know? There was a first time for everything. And she sure *felt* as if she were having a real experience. Fake documents or real, Elizabeth's journalist's instincts had kicked in convincingly enough. She felt as wired and excited as if she were tracking a real story. Maybe there was something to this after all. There was only one way to find out.

She snatched a file from the cabinet—the one on American conspiracies. With a gasp she spotted a yellowed document bearing the chilling heading Assassination: JFK.

"Wow." Elizabeth's hand trembled as she touched the brittle pages. It certainly looked real. And it felt real.

So maybe this is—

Her thoughts were cut short. She froze, dropping the pages to the floor. Someone had tapped her on the shoulder.

And it felt real.

Patman, the president is counting on you . . . and so are the people. . . .

These words replayed through Bruce's mind like a broken record as he set his jaw and moved forward. The task at hand was difficult. Impossible, even. The chances of recovering the stolen microchip were slim to none. But someone had to try, and the U.S. government hadn't hesitated to call Bruce to action.

The choice had been unanimous, the CIA bureau chief informed Bruce in clipped tones. "We know that if we have even the remotest chance of tracking this thing, you're our only hope. You can't let us down, Patman."

Of course, Bruce had hesitated. Although danger was his game, he'd promised Lila he would hold off for a while—let some of the other, lesser secret agents take the heat for a change. Putting his life in jeopardy on a daily basis was affecting Lila's health, and no number of diamond tennis bracelets could comfort her these days. Still, when he'd explained the importance of the mission to her, she'd understood.

So much was riding on this. Without Bruce Patman the United States of America could become history. It only took three brilliant nutcases like Farber, Schweitzer, and von Stercken to devise a plan to access the entire country's nuclear weaponry via the Internet. And it was up to Bruce to stop them.

Sweat beaded down Bruce's face as he screwed up his eyes in concentration. Trying to hold a needle-thin radiothermatic laser beam steady was no mean feat—especially for someone so built. Sometimes huge muscles prohibited extreme delicacy.

Whew! Done!

The vacuum door popped open like a tube of Pringles, and Bruce slid into the lab without a sound. Voilà! There it was, exactly where Bruce had predicted. Hardly bigger than Lila's pinky toenail, the microchip glowed a ghoulish green.

Sorry, dudes!

Bruce grinned wickedly as he popped the chip into a specially designed cuff link. No one could get it now. Then, as quickly and as silently as he'd entered, Bruce left the strong room.

Creeping on all fours through an endless maze of ventilation chambers, Bruce finally found the exit to the main part of the building. Gasping from his grueling tunnel crawl, he felt for his pencil-thin holotorch and sizzled the thick metal grill. In a nanosecond it melted, leaving only a steaming hole, which he pushed himself through. Sweet freedom! But the mission wasn't accomplished. Not quite yet.

Bruce lay panting on the cool grass for a moment, savoring the last few seconds before he struck the final blow against the enemy. He lifted a small black handset from his belt and pushed the glowing red button. Just thirty more seconds and . . . good night, Q-Lab, Inc.!

Boooooom!

A fiery red-orange mushroom cloud exploded into the air, shooting burning debris every which way. Dodging a huge chunk of flaming concrete, Bruce hurled his body onto a rocky verge. The stones bit into his skin, but he didn't even grimace. Pain was part of the deal, and Bruce never flinched.

It was over. No more Q-Lab, with its evil scientists plotting to destroy the free world. Bruce had the chip. The country was in safe hands. And the common man could continue to enjoy his freedom. A tear almost crept to Bruce's eye at the thought.

"Help!"

Bruce leaped toward the source of the distress call. "Lila!"

"Help me!" she pleaded as two men carried her over their shoulders toward a waiting van. Clad only in cherry red Lycra hot pants, a matching halter top, and spiky patent-leather heels, Lila looked as drop-dead gorgeous as always. But mascara streaked her rouged cheeks, and her delicate wrists and ankles were bound with thick rope.

"Terrorists!" Bruce yelled at the two men as they flung Lila into the van and jumped into the front. "Hold on, babe! I'm coming!"

In a flash Bruce was running for his car. "Open sesame!" he yelled. The car roared to life. The door opened, the ignition started, and glowing red lights slid out like insect eyes from the gunmetal gray hood. Bruce's car—the Patmachine—

was one of a kind, specially designed for him by Withers, his own personal gadget man.

Jumping into the front seat, Bruce revved the car and screeched off, climbing from zero to three hundred miles per hour in less than four seconds. Skidding around corners, Bruce took off after Lila's kidnappers like a man possessed. And he was. Possessed by a hatred of evil and the love of his woman.

Cliffs zigzagged past Bruce, but he saw them only out of the corner of his eye. The terrorists were speedy, and although the Patmachine was doing a solid five hundred, the sleazeballs in the van had a good head start.

OK, here goes!

Bruce slammed his foot on the accelerator and clenched his jaw. The car was roaring at optimum speed now, crunching curves and ditches like there was no tomorrow. And there wouldn't be, if Bruce Patman had any say. Not for those Q-Lab criminals.

He was close now. Very close. In his rearview mirror Bruce could actually see steam rising from the tarmac where his tires had burned holes from speed.

Hold on, Li, just one more corner. . . .

Those creeps were going to get it. When Bruce caught up with them, they'd be lucky if they made it to Christmas . . . as stuffing.

"Hey, wait a minute!" Bruce's face clouded in confusion as the road in front of his eyes began to wobble like a mirage. He blinked, but it still looked weird. And then it dissolved altogether. Into static.

"Your CyberDream is now over. . . ."

The screen dimmed to black and Bruce sat back, removing the goggles. His brain was still scrambled from the thrill of his adventure, and it took a moment to fully get himself together.

"Too sweet!" he crowed. Being a supersuave spy was exactly what he'd always fantasized about. Jonah Falk and his CyberDreams certainly hadn't let him down. Sure, it could have lasted a little longer. But hey, there was always next time.

Chapter Six

Please, someone, tell me I'm dreaming. . . .

The stranger's hand lay upon Elizabeth's shoulder. Her skin crawled under its icy touch.

This isn't real! she reassured herself. *This is just a game!*

But she couldn't stop the acrid, dry fear from rising up in her throat like ash. Slowly she forced herself to turn around.

As the face shifted into focus, Elizabeth's stomach constricted in terror. It was a face she knew only too well. The face of her worst nightmares.

The face of William White.

His cold, shining eyes drilled into Elizabeth's. He stood as still as she. His one hand still lingered on her shoulder. With the other he held out a long-stemmed, perfect white rose.

"Is this a joke?" Elizabeth asked, her voice cracking. "Because it's not funny!"

Funny . . . funny . . . funny . . .

Her voice echoed ominously in the large room. But William didn't move, and he didn't say a word. He just stood there, holding out the rose.

"William? If it *is* you . . . what are you doing here?"

Elizabeth's voice quaked with terror. Still William said nothing, although a slight, ironic smile curved at the corners of his full, bloodless lips.

She took a step back. It couldn't be him. It just couldn't be.

"I guess I'm seeing things . . . right?" Elizabeth squeaked. She took another step back, just in case the vision before her eyes wasn't just a vision.

Say something!

But William kept silent. He stood as still as a statue. Not even the white rose he extended moved.

See? Elizabeth tried to reassure herself. *It's just a trick of the imagination. . . .*

Yet no matter how hard she tried to believe her own words, Elizabeth couldn't ignore the fact that what she was seeing looked very real. From his chillingly handsome face with its familiar high, angular cheekbones to his full, sculpted mouth, William was just as real as he'd always been. Even the dewdrops on the petals of the rosebud gleamed an answer to Elizabeth's question. The image in front of her was too real to be an image. Which meant only one thing.

William is alive. . . .

Slowly William lifted his hand, bringing the rose closer to her face. Still smiling, never once taking his eyes off Elizabeth. And as Elizabeth drew a shallow breath of fear, the gentle perfume of the rose wafted to her nose. Seeing might not be believing, she knew. But seeing *and* smelling?

Without wasting another second, Elizabeth wheeled sharply and ran.

"Gather ye round the hearth, for we have supped well and 'tis time to talk of news!"

"Aye! Aye!"

"Aye!" Tom found himself saying. He looked left and right in confusion. He was standing in a tavern with a group of what appeared to be medieval knights. An old, wise-looking geezer with a long, white beard had summoned the group from a spare wooden table to the hearth.

As Tom moved to join the others, he felt as if he were swimming through a sea of mud. Looking down, he realized that he was wearing chain mail, which clinked as he moved. In his hand he also held a shining metal mask.

So I'm a knight? Tom thought excitedly. *Cool!*

"There's a damsel, a bonny damsel. 'Tis said she is from just o'er the way. . . . She hath been captured, only to be lost to us fore'er. . . ."

As the old man continued in a lilting voice, Tom became gradually more transfixed. Maybe it was the roaring fire with its logs oozing sap and popping every few minutes; maybe it was the gravelly tone of the old man's voice. But something about the scene made Tom feel as if he were really in medieval Scotland, sitting around a blazing fire with a mug of ale. It was all so palpable that Tom found it easy to forget who he really was as well as what century he belonged in. And as the old man carried on with his story, Tom was swept away by his words.

I must save this damsel, he thought, leaning in toward the fire. Her face swam before his eyes. He knew her, although the old man had not mentioned her name. She was beautiful Princess Elizabeth, a damsel unlike any other, with flowing golden locks and skin as soft as rose petals. . . .

Within minutes Tom left the other knights to their tales of battle and ran outside into the crisp, dewy air. A high-pitched neigh reached his ears and a broad, gleaming, white stallion trotted toward him. In half a second Tom leaped onto the horse's back and rode off into the night, galloping full force toward Misty Mountain.

The old man had spoken of the damsel being whisked away mysteriously in the dead of night, never to be heard from again. Although Tom could not be certain, he thought he knew where his princess might be. As a knight revered for his true instinct, Tom knew he had to trust his intuition and go on.

"Onward!" Urging his powerful steed up the steep and muddy slope, Tom saw the summit of Misty Mountain appear, rising out of the clouds. The sight chilled him—a long, thin peak, like the bony finger of a witch beckoning him from behind the clouds. *Come!* it seemed to say. *Come if you dare!*

"I shall meet thy challenge!" Tom vowed, digging his heels into his stirrups. "Fear not, fair Elizabeth! I shall come and free thee!"

After a precarious ride along jagged, sheer cliffs and thin paths strewn with loose rocks, Tom arrived at the entrance of a giant cave. A huge boulder sealed off the entrance. There was no one and nothing else in sight.

"Hmmm . . . let's see." Thoughtfully Tom tapped around the boulder, certain he would find something—some way—of opening the portal. But before he had a chance to thoroughly inspect the sealed entry, it opened for him with a massive rumble.

Well, well, well! Tom's eyebrows shot into his hair as the boulder slid away and the dust settled to reveal a dark cave. Just beyond the entryway lay a large, still pool of water. It changed color like a moonstone, lit first an eerie periwinkle blue and then darkening to a deep, glowing mauve.

"Thou knockest . . . and now thou ent'rest!" A voice boomed and echoed around the cave.

"And I would thank thee for thy hospitality"—Tom's voice dripped with sarcasm—"but since thou showest not thy face, I fear thou art trying to deceive me!"

"My face!" the voice roared, followed by a deep, rumbling laugh. "Thou wishest to see my face?"

Suddenly, from just beyond the glassy water, a pair of gleaming red eyes glowed in the darkness, followed by a neck of thick, slimy green scales.

Tom took a step back as the rest of the body emerged—a giant dragon with a tail flickering like a whip, a massive belly, and huge, dripping fangs. In less than a second the giant creature plunged into the water, sending waves crashing through the pool. Then the water stilled.

Where is he? Tom thought in panic, leaning in to scan the surface of the pool. Tom got his answer in a crash and spray of foam as the giant reptile reared up, huge yellow claws flexing, fangs bared.

Almost without thinking, Tom reached for his sword and pulled it from the scabbard on his hip. And as the creature lunged toward him, Tom lifted the shining blade high into the air. "Die, wicked beast!" he yelled.

As a yellow claw the size of a parrot's beak reached toward his neck, Tom closed his eyes and plunged with all his might.

The creature fell back with an almighty howl, and Tom had just enough time to withdraw his sword and spot the damage he'd done: a wide slit the size of a mail slot, which oozed dark black fluid. The creature let out a ragged moan and dropped into the pool, sinking until Tom could no longer see it.

"There!" Casually Tom slid his sword back into its sheath and put his hands on his hips. The dragon had been a bit of an obstacle, but then again, dealing with tiresome beasts was all in a day's work for a knight of his caliber. Now it was time to find and free fair Princess Elizabeth. But where could she be?

"Princess!" Tom called and called. Only the sound of his own voice came back to him. He had no other course but to enter the cave and search.

Gingerly Tom stepped around the narrow rim of the large pool until he came to a dark hole beyond. Feeling at the walls, he entered the blackness. From a distance a small pinprick of light beamed toward him. He followed it, and it grew in size the closer he came until he reached the end of a tunnel and . . . lo and behold—a rainbow!

Dazed, Tom moved through the opening and found himself in a small wooded copse humming with bees, giant multicolored butterflies, and flowers of every hue. The rainbow in the sky winked and gleamed, and Tom stood still for a moment, humbled by the enchanting beauty of his surroundings. A glistening waterfall tumbled at his left, spraying him with drops of clear water. To his right, crystal rocks gleamed like opals and diamonds, forming a landscape of brilliant color.

From the boughs of a fragrant orange-blossomed tree a bird trilled a beautiful, haunting melody. Tom craned his neck to catch a glimpse of the delicate creature, but all he could see were leaves and fruit . . . and then a glistening cascade of thick golden hair as a figure darted from beyond the tree.

"Elizabeth!" Tom called, his heart bursting like a balloon in his chest. "Princess Elizabeth! Don't be afraid! I've come to rescue you!"

The young princess hurried away.

Tom took a step forward and the landscape faded . . . to black.

Wow!

Still half in a trance, Tom removed his headset and blinked. What he had experienced wasn't just his wildest dream—it had been magic!

Tom shook his head in wonder. His CyberDream had been way more powerful and enchanting and exhilarating than even his wildest dreams in real life—daydreams *or* night dreams.

Would he go a second time? Why *wouldn't* he? Tom was more than up for it. A tingle of anticipation fluttered in his stomach. He wasn't sure he could hold out till tomorrow for part two.

Tom stood up and stretched, a faraway smile on his lips. He couldn't wait to find his princess and ask her about her CyberDream. It must have been just as romantic and exciting as his.

*　　*　　*

Help me, someone! Elizabeth pleaded in silent terror. She was too frightened to make a sound. She didn't want to do anything to slow down her sprint.

Her hair streaming behind her, she panted in shallow breaths as bookcases and files whizzed past her eyes. Exhausted, she pushed on, urging herself to run faster and faster. One corridor led to another, then another, with no exit in sight. It was as if the library had turned into a never-ending tunnel of terror.

Is he behind me? She panicked, a white-hot arrow of fear sizzling through her chest like a poker branding soft flesh. But she couldn't stop to look. She had to keep going. She had to get away from that . . . thing.

Picking up speed, she sprinted down the narrow passageway. *Finally!* Her muscles were burning, but her escape hatch was now in sight—a heavy, teak door at the end of the corridor. She fixed her eyes on it, afraid that if she blinked, it would disappear. That door was her only hope for salvation.

You're going to make it! she told herself, trying desperately to believe in her own words. And there was a chance, she knew. If she could just get out of the library, she'd be free. Beyond the terrifying maze of archives and into the open air. Closer . . . closer . . . closer . . .

Every time the door came within her reach, the

corridor would lengthen before her very eyes, stretching and stretching, taking the door farther and farther away from her. She strained to quicken her steps, not caring how painfully her breaths rasped, her muscles burned, or her sides cramped. The ache was more than worth it. She was determined to burn up every ounce of strength she had if she could just leave the library—and William White—behind forever.

Just then the corridor creaked to a stop. Elizabeth yelped as the door suddenly rushed toward her. She stumbled, then slid on the slick floor, bracing herself for the impact.

Suddenly a dark silhouette stepped into her path.

Elizabeth screamed. With a strangled sob she grabbed for the wall to stop herself from crashing into her tormentor. Her heart pounding madly, she closed her eyes, hoping that when she opened them, she would find herself alone.

She didn't.

William took a step forward into a gleaming shaft of light. It illuminated his chiseled jaw, his cold, shining eyes, and the pale rosebud he held out to her.

"Stop!" Elizabeth gasped as William stepped slowly but deliberately toward her. She wanted to lunge past him, but his steady approach already had her backed up against the wall.

William smiled.

"This is not happening!" she cried as William's face swooped down toward hers, his lips nearing her cheek, his hand nearing her chin.

Elizabeth moaned and closed her eyes. She could feel William move his body against hers, pressing her harder to the wall. His lips grazed her cheek.

They were cold.

She screamed.

Suddenly the wall gave way behind her. Elizabeth stumbled backward, breaking William's embrace. But her feet no longer touched ground. She was falling, down and away into oblivion.

"Liz!" Tom shouted as he heard the scream. His heart quickened, and in a second he forgot all about knights and enchanted forests and focused only on the bloodcurdling shriek he'd heard coming from Elizabeth's cubicle.

Quickly Tom sprinted to Elizabeth's booth and ripped away the white curtain. Elizabeth lay sprawled on the ground, completely motionless, the CyberDream goggles still covering her eyes.

For a long, awful second Tom was paralyzed by the sight of her. He knew Elizabeth was in bad trouble. Back in his football days, he'd seen enough accidents on the field to know when someone was unconscious.

"Liz? Can you hear me?" Tom dropped to his knees and ran his hand over her clammy brow, careful not to move her. "Elizabeth?"

The only answer was Elizabeth's shallow, ragged breathing.

Just keep talking, Tom told himself, trying to remain calm as he gently removed the goggles from Elizabeth's head. Her eyes were firmly closed, and Tom knew that wherever she was right now, she was far from him. If he could just get through to her, then she would come to. She had to. She just had to. . . .

Softly Tom stroked Elizabeth's hair and gently repeated her name, but Elizabeth remained impassive. No signs of life but the sound of her breathing and a small, twitching pulse at her neck. "I've got to get help," Tom murmured, fear goose bumping his skin. Several crucial minutes had already passed without a sign of recovery. Tom swallowed hard as desperation seized him. His girlfriend was in grave danger. The situation could be critical.

But just as Tom stood up to run for help, he saw a flickering at her eyelids. He crouched back down again. "Can you hear me?" he asked anxiously, smoothing the hair from Elizabeth's damp forehead.

She turned her head slowly, then began tossing fitfully from left to right, her cheeks drained of all color.

Tom exhaled in a long, sweet release of relief. The situation was by no means good; clearly

Elizabeth was still experiencing some kind of trauma, but at least she was becoming conscious.

"Wake up, Liz," Tom coaxed.

Elizabeth whimpered and mumbled something incoherent before her eyelids finally fluttered open. She stared straight ahead, not seeing him. Her blue-green eyes were glazed over, terrified at first, then confused.

"Where am I?" she murmured, her eyes now skittering from side to side in a panic. She met Tom's concerned gaze and blinked. "Tom?" She furrowed her brow and struggled to get up.

"No! Don't do that!" Tom cried, gently trying to ease her back to the ground.

Elizabeth shook her head and brushed away his hands. "No, really. I'm OK . . . I think." She sat up and pinched the bridge of her nose as if she had a bad migraine.

"What happened to you?" Tom asked, his words coming out in a rush of anxiety. Elizabeth still looked as white as the sheets surrounding her cubicle, and her hands were trembling. He held out his arms to her. "Here."

"I feel so . . . weird," Elizabeth mumbled, sinking into Tom's arms. "I don't know what came over me."

"I think we should call a doctor. You completely blacked out, you know. I'm not sure for how long, but—"

"No. I'm fine," Elizabeth replied quickly. She

shrugged out of Tom's embrace and struggled to her feet, waving off Tom's protests with a shaking hand. "Really, I'm OK. I guess this CyberDream thing just isn't for me," she joked feebly.

"Yeah, obviously not." Tom frowned in concern. "So what happened in here anyway? Do you remember what was going on before you passed out?"

"I don't know. . . ." Elizabeth trailed off. "I guess I just sort of spaced or something. I haven't been feeling that well all day, to tell you the truth . . . classes are kind of burning me out. But I'm fine now. Honestly."

"You don't look fine," Tom replied as he helped Elizabeth out of the cubicle. This was typical Elizabeth behavior, he knew. She didn't like asking for help when she needed it, and she never wanted to make a big deal out of being sick or upset—even when it was obviously a serious matter. Whatever had happened to her in that cubicle—even if it was caused by simple exhaustion—well, Tom could tell that she wasn't going to recover from it anytime soon. She was still shaking like a leaf, and her eyes were wide and alarmed, as if she'd seen a ghost. "Maybe we should call a doctor just to get you checked out," he suggested.

"Tom, please don't do this, OK?" she replied, a little testily. "It's really not necessary. I just need some rest, that's all. I'm just overworked, and this virtual reality thing must have overstimulated my brain. I'll be OK after a good night's sleep."

"If you say so," Tom said. But he remained unconvinced. When was Elizabeth going to learn to accept the fact that all intellectual evidence aside, she wasn't Superwoman? She couldn't pass out for who knew how long, take a nap, and expect to be fine. Still, Tom knew he had to give in. He could be stubborn as a goat sometimes, but he was still no match for Elizabeth in that department.

With his arm firmly around Elizabeth's shoulders, he led her out the tent's exit flap. A few yards away Bruce, Lila, and Jessica were hanging out under the glowing violet sky, laughing and hyperexcited. Not a fainting spell among them, Tom wagered.

"Elizabeth and Tom, finally!" Bruce called out jovially. "We thought you two were never going to come out of there. Hey, we're going to beam ourselves to the virtual Red Lion for a while. Want to come?"

"Thanks, Bruce, but I think we've had a full day," Tom replied, giving Elizabeth's shoulders a reassuring squeeze. "Liz and I are both pretty wiped out."

"Don't be lame, you guys!" Jessica complained. "Please, Liz, you *have* to hear about my dream! It totally can't wait till later."

"It'll have to, Jess. I'm really tired," Elizabeth mumbled.

"Whatever." Jessica shot Tom a withering look before turning to the rest of the gang. "Come on.

Let's get out of here before we get infected with the boredom virus. It's called Wattsitis, and I hear it's pretty catching."

Tom chuckled. "Yeah, you have a good night too, Jess."

As their friends headed for the Red Lion, Tom put a protective hand on the small of Elizabeth's back and steered her in the opposite direction.

"Thanks," Elizabeth added, flashing Tom a grateful smile. "I'm just not up to a big night out."

"Of course you're not, Liz! Are you sure you're OK?" Tom was still a little freaked by the memory of Elizabeth's unconscious body. She did look a lot better now, even if she was still a bit unsteady on her feet. Color had returned to her cheeks, and—thank goodness—she wasn't shaking anymore.

"I'm feeling fine, thanks to you," Elizabeth replied, wrapping her arm around Tom's waist. "You really came to my rescue back there, Tom."

Tom felt a happy warmth spread through his chest, and he kissed the top of Elizabeth's head. *Not bad, Watts!* he thought with a smile. He might not have slain any real-life dragons, but he still managed to save his princess.

Chapter Seven

"Jeez, Lila, I'm just so *surprised* by your CyberDream," Jessica quipped. "Who'd have ever thought that *you,* of all people, would dream of a virtual shopping spree!" Jessica took a slug of her mocha latte and giggled, enjoying Lila's disdainful stare.

"At least Lila's dream was realistic," Bruce retorted with a chuckle. "I mean, *you* rescuing some random dude from a bunch of criminals—now *that's* wild!"

Rolling her eyes, Jessica sighed loudly. Of course, Bruce was way too dense to ever pick up on the fine line between fiction and reality. For him every day was one big frat party, and Jessica knew that for as long as she knew Bruce Patman, he'd be the *last* man on earth to get a clue. If he were even a millionth of an iota smarter, he would realize just how similar cyber-Jessica and real Jessica were at heart. Jessica knew she had it in her to be a top-notch PI just as surely as she knew she had panache. It was the *world*—especially the sleepy little world of Sweet Valley—that was boring, not her!

"I just loved your CyberDream, Bruce," Lila cooed, throwing her arms around his neck and gazing deeply into his eyes. "Saving the country *and* chasing after those dangerous terrorists to rescue me. You're *so* brave!"

"Reality check, Li," Jessica snapped. "It was just a dream, remember?" Jessica leaned back in her chair and closed her eyes. She wished she could remove herself from all of this everyday blahness. Of course, she loved her friends, but they were just so predictable and dull! And lately Bruce and Lila and their cootchie-coo public love-a-ramas had really been getting on her nerves big time.

If only I could live in cyberspace, Jessica thought wistfully. In virtual reality Jessica could be the person she really was, not some shadow of the true Jessica Wakefield. In cyberspace she was free to pursue her natural talents and show the world what a dazzling woman she really was. Unfortunately life was a good few inches more dreary, with pesky chores like classes interrupting Jessica's true self-expression.

Oh, well, at least some *dreams are within my reach,* Jessica mused. If she couldn't spend her days catching criminals, at least she could spend her nights catching Jonah Falk. That part of the CyberDream was totally drawn from reality, she knew. Jessica would easily bet her student loans on the idea that Jonah was just as intrigued by her as she was by him. And even if life at SVU was a bit of a yawn fest these days, luckily Jonah had come along to shake things up a little.

"I just *adore* that I was wearing red in your dream, Bruce," Lila gushed. "But for the record, I would never wear Lycra hot pants. Lycra is far too cheap."

"I'll remember that for tomorrow," Bruce replied with a grin. He squeezed Lila's knee. "Man, I can't wait for part two! I want to see how my dream ends—and how I save my woman."

Jessica suppressed a gag. Bruce could be such a Neanderthal sometimes. Scratch that—make it every single waking minute.

"I can't wait for tomorrow either." Lila's eyes glazed over dreamily. "I wonder what delicious, fabulously glamorous adventures are in store for me. . . ."

Jessica wondered the same thing for herself. She was dying to find out how her CyberDream would end. Of course, she knew whichever way the dream went, it would be spectacular—but the details were still a mystery. Would a helicopter whisk her and Jonah off the roof? Would they find the secret package at the station? Would her stiletto heels survive shinnying up drainpipes? *These* were the questions that plagued Jessica, but none so much as the mystery of the first kiss with Jonah.

How's it going to be? Jessica wondered. *And* when's *it going to be?* She smiled, a shiver of anticipation tickling the back of her neck. Would she get to kiss Jonah first in real life or in cyberspace? The race was on, and Jessica was *so* up for it.

"So then I heard this incredibly beautiful melody, but when I searched for the singing bird, I saw you—well, just your hair, actually," Tom continued, smiling at the memory of Elizabeth's beautiful cascade of blond hair shining in the dappled light of his enchanted forest. "Then it was over. How's that for a beautiful and magical romantic adventure?"

"Hmmm . . . I guess. . . ." Elizabeth frowned, distracted, and began chewing on her thumbnail.

Tom was disappointed. He had hoped that Elizabeth would cheer up when he told her about his CyberDream. But even though she seemed perfectly fine when they sat down on the cool grass of the quad, it took only a few minutes for her to lapse into a strange, abstracted mood. No fairy tales or stories of romantic longing were going to break her out of it, obviously. "Hey, why don't you tell me about your CyberDream?" Tom ventured, trying to keep his tone light and upbeat.

"Not much to say. I told you, I just spaced out

in there. I . . . I don't really remember that much about it, actually."

There was an edge to Elizabeth's voice, and she wouldn't look Tom in the eye. In fact, she'd barely looked at him at all. She'd been glancing over her shoulder every so often. But there was no one else on the quad except for the occasional campus security cop.

"Hey." Tom cupped Elizabeth's chin in his hand, forcing her to look at him. "Why are you so jittery? Would you just relax for a minute, please? You're acting like someone's going to sneak up and attack us any minute now."

"You never know," Elizabeth replied flatly, averting her eyes and scanning to the left of him instead. "It *is* pretty dark out here," she added nervously. "They could really use a few more lights out here on this quad. Have you ever noticed that?"

Tom shook his head in frustration. "Come on, Liz. You're just being paranoid. I promise you, no one is going to mug us or anything." He took Elizabeth's hand and squeezed it for reassurance. "This is one of the safest campuses in the whole country. Look, there's a security cop right over there by the classics building. Nothing bad could possibly happen to us here."

"I suppose so." Elizabeth's tone was doubtful, and she bit her lip.

What was her problem? Tom thought. She really *was* acting weird, as if there were some kind of serial killer lurking on the quad. That could hardly be a side effect of fainting. But as hard as Tom tried, he couldn't imagine what Elizabeth was so freaked out about—and she certainly would have told him by now if it was something realistic and rational. All he could do was keep trying to comfort her.

Elizabeth's head darted to the right. A chipmunk had scurried out from under a bush.

"Honestly, Liz." Tom sighed. "There's nothing to worry about. And as long as you stick with me, you're in safe hands." He tipped her chin up and lightly kissed her lips. "See?"

"OK," Elizabeth replied with a smile. "I'm sorry, Tom. It's just been a long day. And all that virtual reality stuff . . . I guess it really did make me paranoid."

Tom stroked her hair. "So tell me, what *did* you see before your blackout?" he asked gently. "I'm just curious. You don't have to tell me if you don't want to, but—"

"So why do you keep asking me?" Elizabeth snapped crossly. "It was nothing. I was in a big library, that's all."

"A *library*? *That* was your wildest dream come true?" He fell back against the grass and howled. "Jeez, Liz, what kind of fantasy is that? You *already* spend your life in the library!" Tom laughed till his sides ached. "Man, no wonder you didn't want to tell me about it! A library . . . Yeah, that's pretty funny, Liz."

Elizabeth pursed her lips. "It wasn't funny at all," she said softly.

"Of course it's not! You—you *totally* got ripped off!" Tom wiped tears from his eyes. No wonder Elizabeth was so ticked! Despite the look on Elizabeth's face, Tom couldn't stop the eruptions of laughter that kept bursting out of him. So much for Elizabeth's biggest fantasy!

Tom sat up as his fits of giggling subsided. Well, at least now he knew why Elizabeth got so snippy every time he asked about her CyberDream. And if it was anywhere near as boring as the setting, he didn't really need to hear anything more about it. She clearly *was* just exhausted, nothing more. And judging from her current inability to have a sense of humor, she really did need a good night's sleep.

Suddenly Elizabeth gave out a sharp, high-pitched cry and covered her face. Tom jumped, scared out of his wits for a moment. Then he just got annoyed. "What now, Liz?" he asked impatiently. "Did you just remember you have some overdue books to turn in or something?"

Elizabeth pressed a palm to her eye and demanded in a low voice to be taken back to Dickenson. "The stupid wind just blew grit in my eye," she moaned.

"Let me see." Tom tried to move Elizabeth's hand, but she jerked away from his as if he'd just tried to give her the business end of a flaming blowtorch.

"Just take me back, please." She gave him an irritated look. "I want to go. *Now.*"

As Tom led Elizabeth back to her dorm, he stole glances at her face. But her stony expression refused to change.

Tom shook his head. *I give up,* he thought. Maybe he didn't know what kind of stick Elizabeth had gone and sat on. But for her sake, he hoped she would have enough sense to wake up on the right side of her bed tomorrow.

What's going on with me? Elizabeth wondered nervously as she walked upstairs to her dorm room, Tom trailing behind her. She had consciously tried to look calm as Tom walked her home, but she couldn't help the wave of nausea rising up inside her, as thick as mud. And it had nothing to do with Tom's insensitivity. She'd tested his patience, she knew. But she couldn't care less about that right now. All she cared about was what her horrible CyberDream meant.

Jonah Falk had clearly stated the way the technology worked. She was supposed to have envisioned her wildest fantasy. Her CyberDream was supposed to reach down inside her and pull up her deepest subconscious desires. But if that was true, then why did she see William White in her dream?

Elizabeth couldn't make sense of it. Tom had had a perfectly obvious and happy fantasy. So why was Elizabeth dreaming of a twisted psychopath?

A dead *psychopath at that,* she reminded herself. The whole thing was bizarre. Of course she didn't desire to be pursued by William again. The mere idea was as insane as William himself had been. So why was he there chasing her?

A now familiar chill ran through Elizabeth's body as she thought of William's wicked smile. Then all of a sudden it disappeared.

Elizabeth, you are being so *stupid!* she told herself as she headed down the second-floor hall. This whole William thing was nothing more than an illusion. And who cared what Jonah Falk said? What, did he have some kind of virtual Ph.D. in psychology? Please. She'd be surprised if the guy had even graduated from high school. He was just some pitchman hired to make the Virtual Reality Fair sound more impressive than it really was. In *genuine* reality it was just a lightweight concept with a bunch of five-dollar words to back it up. The proof of that was Tom's dream. It was cute, sure, but pretty silly—and hardly realistic.

The image of Sir Tom rushing to save her from an evil dragon made Elizabeth smile. And as she smiled, she instantly felt better—more like herself than she'd felt all day. A teeny sliver of fear was still lodged inside her like a splinter, but Elizabeth had a good idea how to work it out of her system.

She turned around and leaned against the door to room 28. "Come here, Sir Tom," she murmured, grabbing a surprised Tom around the waist. As she tilted her head and closed her eyes to wait for his warm, softly reassuring kiss, Elizabeth felt a million miles away from her awful CyberDream.

This is what I need, Elizabeth thought blissfully as Tom's lips touched her own. A low moan escaped his throat, and he threaded a hand through her hair. *This is what I want. . . .*

Elizabeth kissed Tom back with all the force she could muster, anchoring herself to the moment. *This* was reality. And it felt amazing. Relief flooded her entire body as she felt the comforting pressure of Tom's hands on her waist. This was the man she loved, and his was the face she dreamed about. She opened her eyes and tilted her head to look into Tom's loving—

Blue eyes!

Elizabeth stumbled backward, gasping as she found herself looking into the icy, twin pools she knew only too well. These eyes were nothing like Tom's. Tom's eyes were warm and brown, always simmering with intelligence and passion. These were the eyes of true evil—cold, yet burning with the passion of madness and a keen, wicked brilliance.

William. Again.

With a soft cry Elizabeth closed her eyes and opened them again, just in case it wasn't true, just in case she was just hallucinating.

She was.

Tom's brown eyes looked back into Elizabeth's own, bearing a look of love mixed with bewilderment. He couldn't have missed Elizabeth's abrupt move from embrace to escape.

"Tom," Elizabeth whispered. She didn't think she could feel more grateful for that simple, one-syllable word. *Of course it's Tom,* she chided herself. It had been Tom all along . . . right?

"What did I do wrong?" Tom sighed and flipped onto his back. It was still way too early to go to sleep, so he'd been lying on his bed for the last twenty minutes, trying to work out why Elizabeth had pushed him away. He'd thought he had her all figured out earlier, but then she'd gone and surprised him again, first with her sudden and unexpected kiss and then with her sudden and unexpected case of the freak-outs. From passion to . . . punishment. What had he done to deserve this?

Tom knew he hadn't done a thing. And anyway, it was definitely *not* Elizabeth's style to act kooky with him just to prove a point. Elizabeth was always direct when she was angry or disappointed about something. If she had a problem with Tom, she'd just come right out and say it. Although he had to admit, Elizabeth had been acting very strange lately. She was definitely hiding something. But what?

Like she said, she just needs a good night's sleep, Tom told himself, trying to be sensible. Perhaps Elizabeth would be more cheery the next day.

Tom sure hoped so because he was really looking forward to his second CyberDream. And hopefully, if Elizabeth was feeling better, she'd decide to give CyberDreams another chance too.

Tom propped his chin up on his hand and turned in his bed to gaze pensively out the window. The purple clouds were still spread across the sky like giant puffs of grape-flavored cotton candy. Maybe a fun CyberDream would improve Elizabeth's overall mood. Tom certainly hoped so. All she needed was a good one . . . hopefully one about *him* next time.

Logically Tom knew he shouldn't be hurt that Elizabeth's dream hadn't been about him. It was just a game, after all. But still . . . why would she fantasize about a library and not her own boyfriend? Evidently Elizabeth was way overworked if she was even *dreaming* about libraries.

Maybe she's totally burned out, Tom reflected, a sharp arrow of worry causing him to clench the muscle in his jaw. Well, when it came to studying, there was never anything Tom could do to stop her. All he could do was wait and see how she felt tomorrow.

As Tom closed his eyes, he settled back into his pillows and drifted back into the hazy memory of his fantasy. *My beautiful Princess Elizabeth,* he thought as a flicker of blond hair flashed through his mind. Sure, she had hurried away from him at the end of his CyberDream. But once he caught up to her, she'd see that he was her knight in shining armor—literally. She'd never run from him again.

With a frustrated groan Tom turned onto his side. Would his virtual Elizabeth turn out to be different from the real Elizabeth? Probably. In fact, deep down he hoped she *would* be different. His Princess Elizabeth would never jump away from his kiss. And she would never hide anything from her knight. . . .

This bed is as cold as a grave, Elizabeth thought as she pulled her comforter up to her chin. She couldn't stop shivering. The air in her dorm room was strangely chilly, even though outside it was a humid night. As Elizabeth tried to stop her teeth from chattering, she also tried to stop the wild, morbid thoughts racing through her mind. She couldn't help it, but as she lay in bed, she felt as if she were in a coffin, the black night air around her as thick as damp soil. . . .

Stop it! Elizabeth scolded herself. *You're just overtired!* She knew there was nothing that unusual about the night. She was in the same old bed in the same old room. Maybe a chilly wind had simply gusted through her window. That would make sense—after all, the weather was hardly behaving predictably.

And yet Elizabeth couldn't reassure herself. No matter what she did, she couldn't help the strong sense of foreboding washing over her like an icy blast from the Arctic. And she couldn't help sensing a presence around her. Something cold and forbidding. And familiar.

He was out there. There was no mistaking the rhythmic thud of his footsteps, distant at first but growing closer and closer, leaving their ghostly echo in the hallway outside.

He was coming to get her.

Petrified, Elizabeth could only lie quaking beneath her comforter, the corner of a pillow pressed against her mouth. *Don't scream,* she ordered herself. Perhaps William would leave if he thought she wasn't home.

The footsteps paused. He was outside the door of room 28 now. Elizabeth waited in an excruciatingly long, slow-motion second that unraveled and stretched into what felt like an hour. She squeezed her eyes shut, waiting for the familiar, sharp knock that would surely come. How many times before had she heard that sickening sound—the sound of William's pursuit? Elizabeth couldn't even begin to count how often she'd stood terrified on the other side of that door, waiting for William to leave, only to find a fresh, white rosebud in the hall outside. . . .

What? No! Elizabeth shot up in her bed as if she were attached to a spring. The sound was unmistakable—the silvery clink of keys scraping at the lock. Or perhaps a knife. In an awful, sickening moment Elizabeth realized she was trapped. And as the slow, deliberate footsteps came toward her, she heard them as clods of dirt raining down on her coffin lid.

She was alone.

And he knew it.

Instinctively she filled her lungs, opened her mouth, and screamed.

"Whoa, girl! What's up with you?" Jessica flicked on the overhead light and folded her arms, surveying Elizabeth quizzically. Meanwhile a neighbor pounded on the wall, the traditional Dickenson "keep it down in there" signal.

Whew! Elizabeth ran a shaking hand through her hair and flopped back onto her pillows. "I'm sorry, Jess. I guess I just . . . had a nightmare."

"No need to get your undies in a bunch. It's just me—Jessica Wakefield, PI." Jessica bounded onto Elizabeth's bed, a glint of excitement in her eyes.

"PI? Wha—" Elizabeth choked on her words and swallowed, hoping her voice would get back to normal. "Uh, what's that about?"

"It's the name of my game, lady. It's a tough world out there, but the tough can handle it."

"Huh?" Elizabeth was confused, still shaking and slightly disconcerted by Jessica's obviously chirpy mood. As Jessica began to babble about her CyberDream, Elizabeth couldn't help feeling a twinge of annoyance rising up inside her. There she was, terrified out of her skull by her CyberNightmare, while Jessica was practically levitating with excitement. It didn't seem fair, and it didn't make sense.

"So tell me about yours," Jessica demanded after a long, breathless explanation that Elizabeth could barely understand, including something about flirting with that Jonah guy while escaping gun-toting criminals.

After such an exciting ride Elizabeth knew that telling Jessica she'd spent her precious virtual time in a library wouldn't exactly go down well. And she *definitely* wasn't about to tell her what had happened while she was there. She didn't even know what had happened herself. Glumly she averted her eyes from Jessica's inquiring stare. It was all too much. Elizabeth just wished the Virtual Reality Fair would go away.

"C'mon, Liz. What was your CyberDream about?"

"I'm too tired right now, Jess. I'll tell you tomorrow, OK?"

"Oooh, you're afraid to talk about it!" Jessica squealed. "I can totally tell. I bet it was sex-ee!"

Elizabeth shook her head. "Hardly. Just let me get to sleep, all right?"

"I thought you were already asleep."

"Whatever. Good night, Jess."

After one last moment of pestering, Jessica reluctantly left the room, her basket of bathroom necessities in hand. Alone again in the dark, Elizabeth pulled her covers back up to her chin and sighed. It was just too weird that *everyone* had had so much fun at the Virtual Reality Fair. *Everyone except me,* Elizabeth reminded herself. Maybe the machines were tampering with everyone's minds. If so, then CyberDreams definitely needed to be more thoroughly checked out. What if someone else had as bad an experience as hers? Or maybe CyberDreams were brainwashing everyone on campus!

She sat up, her mind racing in alarm. Then after a moment good sense told her she was just jumping to yet another wild conclusion. Maybe she had just gotten unlucky. In fact, maybe she should give CyberDreams another try before she decided for sure that something sinister was going on. Once she put her emotions aside and looked at the situation from a cool, dispassionate journalist's perspective, that seemed like the best course of action. Maybe next time around it wouldn't be so bad.

Maybe . . .

The word echoed in her mind and then, before she could give it further thought, Elizabeth's eyelids grew heavy from exhaustion, her brain dulled from too much analysis. She fell into a deep, dreamless sleep.

Chapter Eight

"It's nine A.M., people!" Bruce bellowed. "Come on, let's get this party started!"

Impatiently Bruce paced around the tent a third time. Still he found no signs of life. He was early, he knew. About three hours early. Most of the campus was probably still asleep—everyone but the SVU Tai Chi club, who were practicing their moves on the far side of the quad. He could barely believe his eyes—and it wasn't just because the sky was still all freaky looking from the day before. Who at SVU could sleep when the amazing Virtual Reality Fair was right there? And within walking distance, even?

Bruce scratched his head. He couldn't remember the last time he'd gotten up so early on a Saturday morning. Usually he was sleeping off a kegger—if he wasn't still up and partying from the night before. But this weekend things were different. Bruce's

CyberDream was waiting for him, and he had absolutely no intention of being anything but first in line.

Obviously he shouldn't have worried. He already knew he was the only guy at SVU thirsty for heart-pounding adventure, the lone BMOC who lived more for thrills than for books. He easily could've slept in an extra half hour or so *and* had a cup of coffee. Not that he really needed it. After a few loud yawns Bruce felt wide-awake and eager to get into the tent. He was dying to see where his dream would take him, and not even a lazy Saturday morning could tempt him away from the game.

"Hey. You're early."

"Jonah! Duuude!" Bruce grinned as a sleepy, tousled Jonah stepped out from behind the tent flap. "You bet I'm early. I'm raring to go!"

"We don't open till twelve," Jonah replied before taking a slug from a plastic-foam cup. "Why don't you grab some coffee and I'll hold your place for you?"

"Coffee? Nah, I'm wired enough as it is! I've got to get into that tent, save the US of A *and* my girl, man. The stakes are high!"

"Sounds like you had a wild ride."

"The wildest. The coolest!" Bruce enthused. "So wild and so cool that I skipped the java this morning. I'm *totally* running on adrenaline. I'm *pumped!*"

"That's what we like to hear." Jonah chuckled. "A guy who knows how to get into it. A guy who appreciates excitement and adventure. A real man."

"Dude! That's me!" Bruce clapped once and swaggered in place. "Now all I need from you is my headset. Think you can swing that for me, pal?" Bruce shot Jonah an earnest, pleading look.

"We-ell." Jonah glanced back toward the tent doubtfully. "I'm not really supposed to open up before the scheduled time. Company policy, you know?"

"Yeah, right. Anyway, you won't *really* be opening if you just let me slip in unnoticed," Bruce wheedled, wondering if he should reach for his wallet. He wasn't really sure if he should offer up a bribe, but Jonah looked like the type of guy who would go for a nice cash reward—kind of shifty, a little on the scuzzy side. Heck, if Jonah hadn't been affiliated with CyberDreams, Bruce doubted he'd give him the time of day.

Definitely not frat material, Bruce thought, *but he's the man in charge.* He put a hand on the wallet bulging from his jacket pocket, but Jonah didn't seem to take the hint. Maybe he wasn't being obvious enough. But just as he was about to spring for a crisp fifty, Jonah nodded and motioned him in.

"OK, uh . . . what's your name?"

"Patman. Bruce Patman," he replied in his smoothest James Bond tones.

"Ah, yes, Patman. I can tell you're a man of means. A man with imagination and intelligence. A man who knows what he wants and goes for it."

Bruce puffed out his chest. "So I've been told."

For a moment Jonah ran his hand over his

stubbled chin thoughtfully. "OK, Patman." He held open the tent flap. "I'll do you a favor. But it's just between you and me, OK? We'll call it . . . a gentlemen's agreement."

"Excellent!" Bruce could hardly contain himself as he leaped into the tent.

"Ah-ah-ah." Jonah held out his hand. "Still gotta pay admission, pal."

"Oh, of course. Heh—sorry." Bruce fished a few bills out of his wallet and pressed them into Jonah's hand before rushing into the same cubicle he'd been assigned the previous night. That Jonah dude wasn't such a bad guy after all, Bruce realized. He was a topflight salesman running an A-1 business. And if Bruce's CyberDream part two turned out to be as much of a trip as part one, maybe he'd give the guy a nice fat tip.

"Hi, handsome. Are you waiting for someone, or may I join you?" Elizabeth shot Tom a dimpled smile and slid into the booth seat opposite him at the Red Lion.

"You're chipper this morning." Tom grabbed Elizabeth's hand as the waitress put a steaming cup of coffee on the table.

"I'll take one too, please. And the Saturday special," Elizabeth told the waitress, who nodded and walked away. "Tom, I feel *so* much better," she cheered as she squeezed his hand warmly. And it was true. A night of deep, dreamless sleep had done her a world of good, and she'd woken up feeling refreshed, revitalized, and totally her old self again.

Nothing like decent rest to give you a whole new perspective, Elizabeth thought, grateful to see the sun peeping out from the dark clouds that still clothed the sky in a blanket of purplish gray. The weather might not have completely cleared, but the sun was a good sign, and it mirrored the cheerful optimism she felt inside. And as the waitress brought Elizabeth's coffee and a warm chocolate croissant surrounded by fresh raspberries, she dug in, feeling unusually ravenous. *Another good sign!* she thought happily.

It was amazing how different everything looked by the light of day. And after the silliness of the previous day's events, Elizabeth couldn't help marveling at her change of attitude. Tom had obviously also taken notice—and followed suit. He looked more relaxed and cheerful than he had in ages.

"I'm glad you're feeling better, Liz." He reached across the table and tucked a stray strand of hair behind her ear, letting his hand linger for a moment on her cheek. "You really had me scared yesterday."

"All in the past," she assured him. Sitting across from Tom, his loving brown eyes smiling down at her, Elizabeth wondered how she could ever have doubted their relationship or her own grip on her sanity.

Imagining William White, of all people, stalking her *again*—that was just too out there, even for virtual reality. Obviously a simple technical explanation lay behind the whole unfortunate experience. There had probably been a random computer glitch, and what should have been fun had turned into something scary. Maybe by accident the computer had tapped into her worst nightmare instead of her wildest dream. More likely it was the product of an overworked and exhausted imagination. Whatever the reason, it was just a random, one-time experience and certainly nothing to get worked up about.

"Hey, did you forget to kiss me hello or what?" Tom teased, faking being hurt.

"Sorry, honey, I was just so starved!" Elizabeth leaned over the table and cupped Tom's face in her hands. Suddenly, a split second before her lips made contact with his stubbled cheek, an image of William swam into her mind and she hesitated . . . but only slightly.

Planting a firm kiss on Tom's hazelnut-flavored lips, Elizabeth sat back and looked at the handsome face smiling back at her. Just her Tom, nothing—and no one—more. *Of course!* Elizabeth wanted to kick herself for even allowing William to spring to mind, but she let her annoyance pass. She had no more time for that. Stressing over a dead, psychotic stalker was a sheer waste and made absolutely no sense anyway.

"So . . . are you going to try the CyberDream thing again?" Tom queried hesitantly, evidently a little nervous that his question might get shot down.

Elizabeth merely smiled and shrugged. "I guess I might. Could be worth a second try."

"Really? Liz, that's awesome!"

"Slow down, sweetie." Elizabeth laughed as Tom practically shot out of his seat with enthusiasm. "I haven't given a definite yes. . . ."

"Aw, come on," Tom wheedled. "It'll be fun! Maybe this time you'll dream of me . . . on a desert island or something, wearing palm leaves for clothes. Or less." He winked and shot Elizabeth an over-the-top sexy, smoldering male-model look. "Please, Liz. For me?"

"Oh . . . OK!" Elizabeth threw up her hands in mock defeat and laughed as Tom leaned over the table to fold her in a bear hug. "Tom! You'll knock over the coffee!"

He kissed her forehead and sat back. "Spilled coffee? Who cares! I'm just so psyched that you're going to give it another shot, Liz. After what happened to you yesterday, I was so afraid. . . ."

As Tom talked on, Elizabeth felt her thoughts slipping to the familiar territory of cold, hard analysis. In a way, despite her cheery mood, she could still feel deep anxiety simmering under the surface of her consciousness. Rationally she knew she was just being stupid. But the thought of putting that headset on again gave her a pinprick of fear that was hard to ignore.

What if I see William again? she wondered nervously.

You won't! her inner voice countered.

But in her bones, Elizabeth wasn't entirely sure. Which was why she knew she had to go back—to be a hundred percent certain that he was really six feet under the ground. Yes, that was the real reason she was going back again . . . wasn't it? She didn't want to see William White *again* . . . did she?

"I know you're just going for me, but you're going to love it, Liz—you'll see!" Tom glowed happily as he tossed back the last of his coffee.

Elizabeth tried to look equally excited, but it was an effort. As she looked at Tom, she couldn't help feeling a little dishonest. She didn't like keeping the truth from him, but it was necessary. If there was one person, dead or alive, whose name Tom never wished to hear again, she knew it was William's.

I'm sorry, Tom, Elizabeth said silently, feeling a slight tug at her insides. *I hate lying to you, but if you knew why I was really doing this . . .*

She never finished her thought. Tom's lips met her own, and all thinking was suspended for a brief but blissful moment.

"Gotcha!" Bruce sped around the treacherous curve in the Patmachine only to find that the van he was chasing—with Lila in it—had totally disappeared!

"Darn!" Slowing to the snail speed of one hundred miles per hour, Bruce arrived at a crossroads. One road led out of the mountains. The other disappeared into the canyons.

"Now what?" Bruce groaned. Just then he heard a high-pitched, insistent beep. Glancing at the dashboard, he spotted a small liquid-crystal computer screen lighting up. A nanosecond later a map appeared, detailing the region. A small moving dot blinked at him, and Bruce grinned.

Lila's tracking necklace! He'd almost forgotten the supersonic, digitally sensitized high-tech device hidden in a ruby the size of a robin's egg. This was going to be a cakewalk!

Bruce smiled triumphantly as he gunned the engine and took the road that led away from the mountains. In seconds he arrived at the source of the beeping—a deserted aquarium.

"Fish World," Bruce read from a rusty sign as he jumped out of the car. "So *that's* where these schmucks hide out. Clever. Very, very clever. But not clever enough for Bruce Patman!"

Using his laser holotorch, Bruce snapped the padlock on the gates in no time. Once he was inside the cavernous warehouse, things got a little trickier. Lila's tracker distinctly indicated that she was on the first floor, but all Bruce could see were huge, slimy, waist-high tanks of water.

This one's still running, Bruce thought with wonder as he spotted a school of evil-looking piranhas swimming past in the only clear blue aquarium. *I wonder what they live on. . . .*

A chill ran through him as he spotted bones lying in a pile on the floor of the tank. Just as

Bruce was about to answer his own question, he heard an evil laugh. Through a side door he spotted a tall, rail-thin man clad in black, a long silver ponytail brushing his waist.

Gunther Hermann! Bruce recognized the creep—he was Q-Lab's chief thug, the man who took care of Farber, Schweitzer, and von Stercken's less scientific tasks.

"Vellcome to our humble home, Meestar Patman." Hermann stepped toward Bruce, a small, golden Glock glinting in his hand. "Not bad, eh?" With his free hand he pointed at the piranhas. "Wery hahngry," he added, howling with laughter.

"What's this one for?" Bruce gestured at an empty aquarium adjacent to the piranhas.

"Qvestions, qvestions . . ." Hermann slid up to Bruce and seized him roughly by the wrist. "Vhere you're going," he snarled, "you'll haff no need vor qvestions!"

Before Hermann could react, Bruce whipped out his hand and chopped at Hermann's hand in a neat, single blow, forcing him to drop the gun.

"Nice move, Patman," Hermann growled, holding his wrist in obvious agony.

"Clearly you have forgotten I hold a fifth *dan* in *chan shou do,* a particularly deadly style of kung fu," he boasted. "My body is a temple, Hermann. A temple of *danger.*"

Bruce wrestled the man to the floor. Although Hermann was strong, he was no match for Bruce.

He picked Hermann up like a toothpick and flung him into the empty glass aquarium. At that moment Bruce noticed a second gun, presumably pulled from a shoe, which Hermann positioned, cocked, and prepared to fire!

"Sorry, dude!" Bruce seized the large pump in the piranha tank and thrust it into Hermann's tank. Instantly it filled with water—and hungry, carnivorous fish.

Hermann's cries were garbled and muted by the sound of a million gnashing teeth. In minutes all that remained was a slender skeleton, falling softly to the bottom of the aquarium.

"So *that's* what they eat, huh, sleazebag?" Bruce chuckled, an icy-cool rush flooding his insides, his body as light as air. He felt as if nothing could touch him. He was invincible. He was the *man!*

Bruce swaggered toward the small door Hermann had entered from. He pushed at the door and it swung open, revealing a small dusty office and . . .

Lila! Bound, gagged, and trembling, Lila still looked incredibly beautiful. But her tear-streaked cheeks tugged at Bruce's heart, and an anger hotter than volcanic lava rumbled through his insides. "They can't do this and expect to get away with it!" he roared, kneeling down to free Lila's ankles from the rope that bound them.

"Oh yes, we can . . . and will!"

Bruce looked up to see his worst enemy—the evil Dr. Farber. Before Bruce could formulate a witty response, something that felt like an exploding comet hit the side of his head. He slumped to the floor. . . .

The next thing Bruce knew, he was coming to in the empty room—no Lila, no Farber. "Dang, Patman, you screwed up royal!" he scolded himself.

Suddenly he heard a quiet and insidious hiss coming from behind him.

Turning, Bruce almost jumped out of his skin as a mottled lime-green-and-black snake reared up at him, its pink forked tongue flickering.

And now I'm done for! Bruce thought in fear, knowing he had to keep perfectly still. *Maybe if I just slowly inch my hand into my pocket. . . .*

A bead of sweat trailed down Bruce's jaw as he concentrated on keeping as much of his body as still as possible. Meanwhile he reached back and fished into his back pocket, moving his fingers agonizingly slowly. There—he'd found it. Pay dirt.

"Say cheers, Charlie." Bruce whipped his hand out from behind him and blasted his laser pen so the white heat blazed right between the snake's small black eyes. In a second the snake was no more than a pile of sizzling skin. But there was no time to celebrate. No, more tough work lay ahead, and Bruce couldn't afford to waste another second before he had Lila safely in his arms.

"I'll find you, you cowardly slugs!" Bruce vowed, kicking a crate in anger as he pictured the terrorists gloating somewhere. Bruce knew they were long gone by now, and all he could hope was that Lila's necklace would lead him to her. It all depended on how far away they already were—and judging from the woozy feeling in his skull, Bruce figured they'd had at least a half hour to make their getaway. That was a dangerous advantage.

But I'll find you, babe. Bruce closed his eyes, sending Lila his mental message. When he opened them, all he saw was darkness. "Your CyberDream is now over. . . ."

"Over!" Bruce was livid. "But . . . but . . . but how can it be over? I haven't found Lila yet!"

Bruce threw his headset to the ground and left his cubicle. He'd paid his money, and now he'd been left hanging. Well, Bruce Patman was one man who did not stand for unfinished business. Health risks or no health risks, he'd just have to go again.

"I'm so megapsyched, I can barely stand it!" Jessica squeezed Lila's arm as they neared the CyberDreams tent. "This whole experience is just so . . ." Jessica struggled for a word to adequately describe the thrill she was feeling. "It's just so . . . mega," she finished weakly.

"I can't wait," Lila replied. "I was up practically all night."

"Me too!" Jessica squealed.

"Lost beauty sleep. This better be worth it."

"Oh, puh-*leeze,* like it's *not?*"

Lila squinted and touched the tips of her fingers

to the corners of her eyes. "Actually, I think this whole experience is giving me crow's-feet. Look, Jess. Do I have crow's-feet?"

"Jeez, Li! Of course not!" Jessica said before inspecting Lila's lids. "Well . . . maybe a little."

"Ohmigod!" Lila shrieked.

Jessica snorted. "Kidding!"

"You stink, Jess."

Jessica skipped a few steps. "I am so beyond excited. My stomach is going crazy." And so was her heart. A dreamy sigh escaped her lips as she spotted Jonah in the distance. Even though he was a ways from her and she couldn't yet make out his chiseled features, she was already dizzy with lust.

"Love struck, are we?" Lila observed saucily. "I thought you'd sworn off the stuff."

"I never said that," Jessica replied haughtily. Why did Lila always take everything she said so literally? Groaning with exaggerated impatience, she turned to Lila and spoke as if she were trying to explain to a child why clouds were white. "I never said I was through with *men;* I just said I was through with *fools.*"

"Hmmm . . . I could have sworn you said something about taking your time before falling for the next guy," Lila replied pointedly, trying unsuccessfully to suppress a knowing smile.

"And I did . . . I am," Jessica finished lamely.

"Admit it, Jess, you threw that idea out the window in two seconds flat."

"Yeah, I guess you're right. I did. Kind of like you with your New Year's resolution to quit watching the Home Shopping Network," Jessica jibed.

"Well, at least we both get to live out our dreams now—in cyberspace *and* in reality." Lila nudged Jessica as they neared Jonah, and the two fell into a comfortable silence as they wandered toward the line, Jessica absorbed in fantasies about where her CyberDream might take her next while Lila looked starry-eyed, dreaming—Jessica imagined—of exotic cruises aboard floating fashion emporiums.

"Uh-oh, crash landing nine o'clock," Jessica muttered as Alison Quinn came out of the CyberDreams tent. "Not a nice way to greet the day," she whispered as Alison nodded coolly in their direction.

"Did she have to come back?" Lila moaned. "Eew, she's probably contaminated my cyberspace!"

"Like she's even *capable* of imagination," Jessica drawled. "That wench is about as deep and interesting as a birdbath."

"I bet she dreamed something really disgusting," Lila remarked as Alison walked stiffly across the quad. "Look at her. If she were any more uptight, she'd explode."

"Now *that's* a CyberDream," Jessica replied, sending herself and Lila convulsing into a giggling fit. "I bet you're right," Jessica added when she finally caught her breath. "Whatever she dreamed must have been pretty gross."

"Like forcing all the Thetas to clean her room

and clip her toenails. Ugh! Or maybe making out with that total goober from *Saved by the Bell* . . . you know the one, the guy who . . ."

Lila kept on babbling, but Jessica soon lost all interest in Alison. Why waste her energy on dissing that withered freak when she was only a few feet away from Jonah and a few minutes away from her next CyberDream? A pleasurable tingle shot up from Jessica's toes right up to the roots of her hair.

Not long now, she thought excitedly. *And not long for you either, my pretty!* She sighed as she watched Jonah taking admission and handing out tickets, his trim, muscular arms and wide shoulders filling out his black T-shirt quite nicely. Yep, Jonah Falk had a date with destiny . . . and Jessica Wakefield, PI!

This is nice . . . , Elizabeth thought dreamily as she gazed around her. Nothing but wispy white clouds stretching into the horizon like threads of gossamer from a never-ending bolt of cloth . . .

Feeling as light and airy as a cloud herself, Elizabeth took a step into the blank wilderness unfolding before her and then, out of nowhere, a shape moved into focus and stepped up to block her.

William White.

Elizabeth's throat constricted, cutting off her scream. It felt as parched as an Arizona desert. She tried to swallow, tried to protest, but she could only stand numbly as William held out a white rose and opened his mouth to speak.

"Elizabeth . . ."

His voice was soft and husky, not at all like the harsh, crazed voice she remembered. And his face looked different too—softer somehow, although his aristocratic bone structure still gave him a haughty look. Perhaps it was his eyes. . . . He looked at her gently, almost pleading.

For forgiveness? Elizabeth couldn't be sure, but she somehow felt soothed by the way he was regarding her. He seemed tentative, sweet, even, like the William of long ago. The William she once knew before the craziness had set in.

"Liz, please. If you'll just give me a chance. Don't be afraid," William whispered, taking Elizabeth's hand and gently pressing the rose into her palm. She expected to feel sharp thorns prick her skin, delivering the sting that inevitably drew blood.

She felt nothing. Nothing but a bizarre sense of safety, of calm . . .

"N-No . . . I can't," Elizabeth stammered, dropping the rose. "I can't go through with this. I don't *want* to—"

"You're so lovely, Elizabeth," William murmured, his eyes burning with intensity. A benign intensity suggesting warmth and gentleness rather than obsession. "I don't know how I can prove myself to you," William continued in a subdued tone, "but if you would only let me love you, I know I'd never let you down. You're a rare gem, Liz. You're the rose among thorns."

"I . . . must go," Elizabeth replied weakly, trying to look away. But William's crystal gaze locked onto her own, and she found it impossible to look away.

"It's all been a terrible misunderstanding," he continued, undaunted. "If you only knew what I've been through. And losing you, Liz—that was the worst. . . ." William looked genuinely sorrowful and tender, his eyes not wavering from Elizabeth's. "But you're back now," he added, a grateful smile forming on his full lips.

"I'm not. And you're lying," Elizabeth retorted feebly. She couldn't help herself. Something deep inside her was softening, yielding to William. She *wanted* to believe his words. They sounded heartfelt, and he looked so sincere and so . . . handsome.

Elizabeth felt her fears slide away as she melted in William's charm—as warm and tingling as the sun on her bare shoulders. She was falling—not literally, not the way that had ended her encounter with him the day before. She was falling under William's spell again. She'd all but forgotten the exhilarating effect he'd once had on her. Now it came back to her as sharply as déjà vu. And there was nothing she could do but ride with it.

I'm really losing it this time, Elizabeth thought as William lifted his hand to her cheek. *And it feels . . . so . . . amazing. . . .*

Chapter Nine

"My stars and garters, get a load of these paparazzi!" Lila exclaimed. She extended a gloved hand to the chauffeur and stepped daintily from the sleek black limo. Her eyes hurt from the gazillion popping flashbulbs, but she knew she wouldn't have to suffer for long. The red carpet was out, and in just a few moments she'd be safely stashed away inside the glittering nightclub.

"Those people are just *dreadful!*" Lila pronounced as Bruce escorted her past a row of jostling photographers.

"I guess the plebs must have their pictures," Bruce replied as he adjusted the jacket of his exquisitely cut, custom-made tux. "All they have are distant fantasies, poor creatures. As for me, my fantasy is right beside me." He slid an arm around Lila's waist and pulled her close. "Just look at you! You're perfect."

Lila blushed as Bruce's eyes roamed all over her body. Clad in one of the new outfits he'd bought for her earlier—a clingy, apple green sequined dress with a plunging V neckline—Lila felt like a queen. No, a goddess. Never had she had such a perfect day, and never had she met anyone near as perfect as Bruce—slightly brooding, intensely adoring, and with a hotness factor to rival any movie star's. Lila silently thanked the heavens for sending her a flawless man.

"You're being so understanding about all of this," Bruce murmured appreciatively as Lila agreed to pose for precisely one second. "I know you hate this tawdry nonsense."

"I do, I do." Lila sighed, flashing her pearly white teeth at the oohing photographers. "But I realize you have a responsibility to the public." She lifted her head and struck yet another dazzling pose as the photographers flocked like pigeons at her feet. It *was* tedious, to be sure, but the press was the press, and Lila didn't think it would hurt to indulge them, especially when she knew she looked ravishing.

As Bruce flashed Lila another tender, grateful smile, she felt her stomach flip like an overexcited salmon. Being with a man of such powerful social standing who—aside from his wealth and influence—could also be loving and sensitive to the needs of the woman in his life was almost too much for Lila to bear.

Wow! As if being with Bruce wasn't enough, Lila's eyeballs practically popped out of their sockets when she and Bruce entered the exclusive nightclub. Champagne flowed from giant tiers of glasses, beluga caviar gleamed from bowls as big as bathtubs, and everywhere she looked, Lila spotted celebrities clad in the finest evening wear. Sure, Lila had witnessed scenes to rival this one countless times, but somehow she felt as if she were seeing it all for the first time, with fresh, unjaded eyes.

Rubbing shoulders with the rich and famous at last! Lila thought, a small tear springing to her eye as she realized she had achieved her childhood dream after many, many years of almost giving up. Finally . . . her kind of people! Quietly Lila had a private, emotional moment as she reveled in her accomplishment and thanked herself for never giving up on her goal despite numerous setbacks among the peasants of small-town Sweet Valley.

"Darling, I'd like you to meet . . ." Over and over again Bruce echoed this line, finishing the sentence with an array of names so famous, no last names needed to be mentioned.

All through the night Lila shook hands with the crème de la crème of the film, art, and fashion worlds, keeping her cool every time to show them that she was at home with them all. No silly shrieks, no requests for autographs or insider dirt on costars and backstage backstabbing. Subdued yet witty conversation was the way to go.

She, Lila Fowler, was finally one of *them*. And judging by the way the men fawned at her feet and kissed her hand, Lila had pulled off a major social coup. And when men handed her their business cards and asked for hers, she was at a loss until she searched her beaded bag and found she actually had some tucked away. Lila F., Faces International, they read. How intriguing! She was obviously a world-famous supermodel! Not at all a stretch, she knew.

And so what if the women were frosty and snotty? *Jealousy,* Lila thought, tossing it off with a shrug of her bare shoulders. Sometimes even celebrities couldn't compete with a young, charming supermodel in an apple-green-sequined Calvano Galina original. It was that simple.

I'm flying. . . . Lila twirled on the dance floor, a little giddy from the combination of too much Dom Pérignon and the heady feeling of being in Bruce's arms, inhaling the manly scent of his expensive, limited-edition cologne. The evening had been a raging success—everything a girl could ever dream of, and as Lila let Bruce sweep her into his arms for a slow number, she thought she might die then and there of total, complete happiness.

"Whoo-hoo! It's my song!" In a second Lila spun out of Bruce's arms and leaped up to the dance-floor podium, all in the time it took for the opening beats of "Private Dancer" to hit the speakers. As Tina Turner began to croon, Lila rolled her hips to the rhythm, oblivious to anything but the sound of the music.

After a moment she heard a roar as if from far away. When she opened her eyes, she saw that every man on the dance floor was clapping and cheering, transfixed by her sensuality, beauty, and stunningly executed moves. As the song drew to a close, Lila beckoned to Bruce and he came up to the edge of the podium, standing at her feet among all the commotion. Neatly Lila performed a graceful pirouette followed by a swan leap, landing delicately in Bruce's arms—and in perfect time to the music too.

"You are a goddess," Bruce whispered into Lila's ear as the crowd went wild.

Feeling exhausted yet thrilled by the evening, Lila was nonetheless happy to be escorted down the red carpet once more and into the waiting limo. As the door closed, she snuggled up to Bruce, enjoying the privacy as the car glided away with barely a purr.

"I know this isn't much compared with what I gave you earlier, Li," Bruce began, "but please accept this humble gift as a token of my tremendous and everlasting admiration."

Bruce snapped open a deep burgundy velvet box embossed with Florentine gold trim to reveal a stunning platinum bracelet festooned with diamonds as big as M&M's and brilliant enough to light up the interior of the dark limo.

"Oh, Bruce . . . you're my prince!" Lila sighed as Bruce snapped the clasp around her wrist. With a smoldering look he leaned in to trace her jaw with the tip of his index finger. As Bruce's mouth found hers, Lila returned his kiss with all the passion she had ever felt in her whole life. She closed her eyes, savoring the moment, and saw sparkles shimmering behind her closed lids, like stray sequins or shooting stars on a magical night. . . .

"Oh, Bruce . . . ," she moaned. Then she frowned in confusion. The glittering stars had somehow become smaller and smaller, and now they were nothing more than a million tiny speckles of gray. What's more, Lila realized, her eyes were open. *Static!* she fumed as the automated CyberDreams voice cut into her reverie. It took Lila a full second to unpucker her lips and a full minute to leave the cubicle. Reluctantly she wandered out of the tent, trying not to feel too disappointed. She knew she had just experienced the dream of a lifetime. But why did it have to end?

Don't believe him! He's a monster!

Elizabeth jerked her head away from William's hand and blinked, her inner voice still echoing insistently from somewhere deep inside her. She stepped back, stunned that she had come to within a hair of being brainwashed by William yet again.

"You're not my fantasy," she snapped, her voice low and shaking with anger. "You're my worst nightmare. And you're history, William, get it? History!"

Confusion clouded William's handsome face, but the soft, pleading look in his eyes remained. "Elizabeth, don't do this," he implored. "I love you. You mean the world to me. Don't deny your feelings. . . ."

As William continued, his voice throaty with emotion, Elizabeth felt the slow pull of his words tug at her as if he were a magnet and she nothing more than a paper clip—light and airy, with no will of her own. It was useless trying to turn away. William's voice was both a balm and a drug, flooding into the very core of her soul, numbing, sweet, and . . .

Deadly! Resist him!

But William's eyes bored into Elizabeth's like twin rays of mellow light, suffused with heat and love. "Just give me a chance, Elizabeth. Just one more chance. That's all I ask."

"Never!" Elizabeth spat, but even to her the denial sounded fake and forced. "I hate you," she added, but again her words seemed as insubstantial as the wispy clouds around them.

"No, you don't. You love me. You've always wanted me. Admit it." William's tone had changed somewhat, had become more insistent. "You've always been attracted to my dangerous side."

Yes . . .

No!

Elizabeth's head was swimming, and she pressed her fingers to her temples to try to clear her mind. But it didn't work. She felt as if she were drowning in a thick fog.

"We're opposites, Elizabeth. And opposites attract. Danger and calm, fire and ice, light and darkness . . ."

"That's true," Elizabeth murmured as William touched her cheek lightly, his gaze scorching her skin. "Yes . . ."

He was beginning to make sense. As Elizabeth felt the heat—yes, *heat*—of William's body pulsing from his heart to the line of fire he traced on her cheek, she closed her eyes and gave in to the forces pulling her toward him. It was as inevitable as an apple falling to the ground. Like gravity or a volcanic eruption, the forces of physics and nature were drawing two opposites together as one in a ritual as old as the universe itself. . . .

It's meant to be.

Elizabeth tilted her chin and closed her eyes, ready for William's kiss. . . .

"Wait! I see a way!"

Jessica grabbed Jonah's arm and sprinted to the edge of the roof. "Don't look down!" She clenched Jonah's hand. Then, inhaling deeply, she took a running jump, pulling Jonah with her.

Graceful yet speedy, Jessica sailed through the

air, her long legs stretching into a perfect split high above the buzzing traffic. Neatly bringing her stilettoed feet together, Jessica landed firmly and safely on the roof of the next-door building, Jonah at her side. There was no time to stop and exhale with relief, however. Jessica could feel the criminals hot on her heels, although she severely doubted they would manage such a daring feat. Still, she wasn't about to stick around and find out.

In seconds Jessica and Jonah slid down a chute and climbed through the first open window. The stairwell. Perfect. Taking to the stairs at the speed of a cheetah on steroids, Jessica fled down to the ground floor with Jonah beside her.

"I've got wheels, don't worry!" Jonah panted. "Wait here." Quick as a flash Jonah returned, revving the engine of a gleaming, jet-black Harley-Davidson.

"You're good, mister."

"Not nearly as good as you, Wakefield." Jonah grinned, and Jessica felt her stomach roll and churn like a washing machine. *Soooo studly!* she thought, admiring the way Jonah's biceps bulged as he lifted the screaming motorcycle and pulled off a perfect wheelie.

Suddenly Jessica stiffened, her spine tingling like a lightning conductor. Footsteps were behind her, urgent and familiar.

"Let's bail!" She bent her knees and sprang with demure determination onto the back of the moving motorcycle, careful not to let her skirt ride up too high.

As they roared off down the boulevard, rain tumbled down in sheets. Even though they were moving faster than bullets from an AK-47, Jessica wasn't worried about wiping out on the slick pavement. They skidded around corners and through stoplights, but Jonah handled it all perfectly, guiding the motorcycle with the precision and power of a pro.

Mmmm, tasty. Jessica sighed and clung tighter to Jonah as she felt his muscles tense with each turn. She nestled her head against Jonah's back, laced her hands even more tightly around his six-pack of abs, and breathed in the smell of leather and fuel, an intoxicating combination that almost drove her crazy with desire.

"Have we lost 'em yet?" Jonah yelled above the wind.

Jessica turned her head, startled. She'd hardly realized they were still being followed. And they weren't—not anymore! She giggled, the taste of victory sweet on her tongue. Wherever they were now, there was no doubt in her mind that those hacks who prided themselves on being pros were way behind, lost in the city streets.

"We're home free!" Jessica threw back her head and howled with laughter, her wet, golden hair trailing behind her. Instinctively she knew it still looked *flawless.*

As they pulled into an empty alley, Jonah slowed to a gentle putter, finally stopping behind a trash can. "Phew!" He ran a hand through his windblown spikes and climbed off the motorcycle. "Now *that* was a wild ride!"

"You can say that again," Jessica murmured, her eyes lingering appreciatively over Jonah's long, lean physique.

"Wakefield, you are one heck of a wild woman!" Jonah declared huskily. Licking his lips, he stepped forward to encircle his arms around Jessica's waist.

"That goes for you too, pal." Jessica leaned into Jonah's embrace, still sitting on the back of the motorcycle. And as Jonah began to kiss the back of her neck, Jessica closed her eyes, oblivious to anything but the warmth of Jonah's soft mouth moving across her neck and up to her jaw. As Jonah's lips sought her own, Jessica felt as if she were sailing through the galaxy on a comet, stars hurtling past her eyes. The last hour of furious, exhilarating action together with a fiery, hypnotizing kiss in the pouring rain left her stunned and delirious from excitement. It was almost overwhelming—even for a woman who packed a custom-designed piece and was known for her wicked ways with men.

After a few more blissful make-out moments Jessica reluctantly pulled away. She'd had enough romance to tide her over till later. Sure, they were out of the hot seat . . . for now. But their lives were still in danger.

"What's wrong, Wakefield?" Jonah asked. "Was that too much for you?"

"Too much is never enough," she quipped. "But you'd better listen up. Something tells me we've gotta bolt outta here but fast. Sooner or later those creeps'll track us down. If they bring reinforcements, we're tuna in the can."

"Gotcha. But where to?"

"Redhill North. The train-switching station. They've hidden something there, and if we get a move on, we could nab it before they do."

Jonah lowered his gaze. His long lashes were dark against his wet skin as he looked Jessica up and down reverently, almost as if he couldn't quite believe how he'd managed to hook up with such a brilliantly gifted siren. "Did I happen to mention how good you are, Wakefield?"

"You did mention it. But call me Jessica."

And call me anytime. . . .

Jessica grabbed Jonah's chin and forced him to look at her. She gazed deeply into Jonah's coal dark eyes until her entire vision became nothing but a pool of black.

"Jonah?"

Confused, Jessica blinked, then sighed as she heard the cool voice of the computer signaling the end of her CyberDream.

"Aw, come on!" she complained. "It can't end

like that! No way!" Jessica stared at the screen to see if she'd somehow missed something.

"Please remember to remove all your belongings. . . ."

"Oh, shut up!" Jessica snapped. She flung off the headset and flounced out of the cubicle. Her eyes flashing with anger, Jessica stalked out of the tent, furious that her CyberDream had ended incomplete. But as she passed by the entrance, Jessica's anger dissolved in an instant. Jonah was still working the line, but his eyes were firmly on her, his intense, seductive gaze identical to that of the Jonah in her CyberDream.

Hmmm . . . Jessica smiled back demurely, but her brain was ticking like a bomb. She slowed her pace and concentrated on sauntering toward the edge of the quad in a slinkier, sultrier way.

Feeling the heat of Jonah's gaze on her back, Jessica felt the thrill of accomplishment right there at her fingertips. Still, she felt tempted to turn around.

Walk away! she instructed herself. *Let him come and get you . . . and he will!* She knew he would. And she couldn't wait. Her CyberDream might have screeched to a premature halt, but the game wasn't over yet! In fact, the games were only just beginning.

Yes . . . we are *meant to be together forever. . . .*

Elizabeth parted her lips slightly, anticipating

William's soft kiss, her mind swirling with a tornado of words and feelings struggling to be heard.

Love . . . you . . . me . . . forever . . . no!

Elizabeth's eyelashes fluttered open and she gazed like a startled bird into William's clear blue eyes, focused and intense.

"Stop!"

Elizabeth's voice quavered, but she took a very firm and decisive step away from William. Her head felt as heavy as a lump of lead, and she fought to keep herself from slipping further under William's hypnotic spell. He was good. He was very good. But Elizabeth could see through him. And she would fight him every inch of the way.

"Elizabeth, don't," William cajoled, placing his hands on her shoulders. "Don't deny our love."

"Love? You don't even know the meaning of the word! You're a cold-blooded reptile!" Elizabeth's voice shook with fury, but William remained calm, patient, undeterred by her anger.

"Just let me hold you," he continued, his voice as smooth as golden honey dripping from a silver spoon.

"N-No!" Elizabeth stuttered, breaking away from William's grip. "Never!" she shouted, bolder now.

But still he kept coming closer, talking in low, sweet tones, murmuring words of love and encouragement. "Just accept the truth, Elizabeth. For the truth is what is meant to be. Accept what fate has preordained for you. Accept me."

"No!" Elizabeth shook her head. It took every effort of will and muscle to move it. She felt heavier, as if her whole body had been dipped into cement, which was now hardening into a thick, stone skin. Still she kept shouting, although her voice sounded distorted and faraway, as if she were trapped in a well. *"No!"*

"I love you," William whispered, reaching out and pinning her arms to her sides.

"No . . . no . . . no!" Elizabeth struggled, feeling herself grow weaker, falling to the ground as William hovered over her.

She saw his face swoop down just inches above her own, his eyes charged with passion. "Let go!" she wailed feebly, her strength waning by the second.

"Never!"

Never. The word reverberated in the air. Elizabeth felt the last remnants of her resistance fading away. Helpless, she grew slack in William's viselike grip. She couldn't even speak. All she could do was *think* the word *no* one last time before everything went black. Then all was still, except for the distant crackle of static that filled her ears. . . .

"Princess? Where are you?"

Nothing. Nothing but rustling leaves, the silvery tinkle of the waterfall, and the lone bird-song, all of which seemed to whisper a secret in a language Tom could not understand. The forest was filled with a sense of knowledge just as surely as it held the promise of magic, but Tom's question died on his lips without the reward of an answer. There was no other option before him but to keep looking. His princess had to be out there somewhere.

With his mighty stallion left behind at the mouth of the cave, Tom took off on foot down a small winding path that led past mountain pools that gleamed iridescent colors under the sprays of tumbling waterfalls. He made his way up a steep bank where huge red-and-white-polka-dotted toadstools pushed up from the thick, rich soil like fairy parasols. He passed strange twisted trees, their limbs gnarled like the fingers on an old man's hand. At last he headed toward the dark thicket of forest that lay beyond, nestled in the valley like an emerald in a shoe. The forest was thick and tangled, so that barely any sunlight made its way through to the ground. Walking in the eerie near darkness, Tom wasn't certain of which direction to head, but somehow he felt drawn to each path he took, as though the princess were guiding him through her spirit.

"And this . . . ?" Tom stopped in his tracks as he noticed a giant tower stretching up before him. It was dark and windowless except for a small hole near the top. *Creepy,* Tom thought, sensing the presence of something sinister behind the forbidding walls.

"A lovely home, wouldst thou not agree, young sir?"

The voice was as cold as an icicle. Tom shivered as he felt icy breath on his shoulder. Turning, he came face-to-face with the ugliest woman he'd ever seen. *If that beast could be called a woman!* Tom thought.

Hunched over, with beady black eyes as small as raisins, a huge hooked nose sprouting hairy growths of immense size, and thin, bloodless lips, the speaker was an old crone.

Now she *puts the* h *in* hag! Tom mused as he recoiled from the foul stench of the crone's breath. He was willing to bet the Holy Grail that this crone knew *exactly* where the princess was. With a sly grin Tom glanced up at the tiny window at the top of the tower. His princess was there. He could feel it in his soul.

"Care to invite me into thy home?" Tom asked in an innocent tone.

"Not a chance. I'd sooner turn thee into a toad!" With that, the hag threw back her head and cackled, a high-pitched hacking noise that made Tom's hair stand on end. Abruptly she stopped and looked Tom up and down, a glint in her eye. "And if thou even triest to get in, thou shall meet thy bitter end, I guarantee, for I am a witch and no one crossest me!"

"Nice rhyming technique." Tom's tone was flat, unimpressed. "Pity about the threat," he added with a yawn. "Doesn't exactly make me quake."

"Oh, really!" the witch spat. "So thou hast no fear, I am to believe?"

"Nah. Can't say I'm buying it."

"Speak English, boy!" The witch was really hopping mad now, which was precisely what Tom had intended.

"Sorry, lady. What I meant to say is: Nay, I hath no fear of thee since I believest not in thy so-called magical powers. Sounds like a crock, if thou askest me!"

"I'll show you!" the witch yelled. Flecks of foamy spittle flew from the corners of her mouth. "Feast thine eyes and open thine ears!" She cleared her throat with a phlegmy cough and began:

> Ho, ho, ho, by my crooked little toe,
> from small to large I wish to grow!
> Hee, hee, hee, by the powers that be,
> Make me as tall as the tallest tree!

Yikes! Tom tried not to show his amazement as a pink-and-orange ball of fire consumed the witch from out of nowhere, crackling and leaping around her but not so much as burning a gray hair on her shriveled head. And then in an instant—*kaboom!* She shot up like a bean sprout, just like the one Tom had seen in a quick-time movie for bio. As if that wasn't enough, the crone then began to expand, puffing out until Tom thought she might burst.

"There!" she boomed, her voice now deep and rumbling. "So much for thy skepticism. An ogre stands before thee now. What dost thou have to say about that, little knight?"

"An ogre? I think thou lookest more like a giant marshmallow," Tom replied, sounding disappointed. "Besides, that kind of magic is old hat. Everyone knows how to do the giant trick. It is rife with predictability. Not at all sophisticated."

"Sophisticated!" the witch screeched, livid. "Name it, fool. I can do it!"

"Big and ugly is easy. I bet thou couldst not turn thyself into something small and beautiful—like a flower, let's say."

"Oh ho! Look who laughs now. That is peanuts, metal pants!" As the witch began to chant more magic mumbo jumbo, Tom couldn't believe his luck. She'd bought it! What a sucker!

Sure enough, the magic worked and within seconds the ogre glowed pink and orange and then disappeared into a cloud of smoke, only to be replaced by a small, bloodred daisy growing quietly in the dust.

"Yeah, look who laughs *now!*" Tom chuckled as he grasped the flower at the stem and yanked it out of the ground. "In thy face, rhino snout! You are his-to-ry!"

He chuckled as he glanced at the flower wilting in his palm and picked the petals off one by one. "Guess I hast not to play the 'she loves me, she loves me not' game with thee, witch! I think I have my answer to that one." Tom tossed the last petal to the ground before crushing the stalk under his boot. Then he looked up and scanned the top of the tower.

"Princess, are you up there?" Tom yelled. No answer came. There was only one way to find out.

In seconds Tom scaled the formidable wall of cement, using metal arrows as hand- and footholds. It was easy. With his bull's-eye archery skills, Tom shot the arrows into place from the ground, and the rest was just muscle and stamina—nothing new for a knight.

"Princess?" Tom called as he slid through the tiny window and stepped into a small room bathed in candlelight. A young woman, her back to the window, sat at a spinning wheel. Her hair was a curtain of gold, not unlike the spun silk at her feet. Even though he couldn't see her face, she was still bewitching and radiant. Princess Elizabeth . . . at last!

"Princess! Have I found thee?" Tom's words tumbled out joyfully. "It is thee, Princess Elizabeth, is it not?"

But Tom received no answer. As he stared at the figure before him, her hair turned suddenly to black.

What? Tom frowned. Suddenly he realized that the candle had gone out. All he could see was darkness. . . .

That's it? Tom cursed and heaved a sigh of disappointment as he removed his headset. It was all over, and just when he was about to see Princess Elizabeth's face. What a bummer.

More than a little annoyed, Tom stepped out of the tent and into the harsh light of day. The real world—ugh. He couldn't believe his CyberDream ended when it did. So much for getting his money's worth. And so much for spending any time with the Elizabeth of his dreams.

Chapter Ten

What . . . happened?

Gasping for breath, Elizabeth turned her head to the side. She was lying on the ground, and something was lodged painfully behind her ear. It was her headset, tangled in her hair. As Elizabeth pulled her hair free of the wires, she felt a slicing pain in her shoulder. It must have made contact with the hard ground.

Gingerly she stood up, her mind seething with disjointed images. Images that were somehow linked, however, like loose pieces of a puzzle: white clouds, a white rose, the white sheets of the CyberDreams tent . . . and William White.

As she recalled how close she'd come to kissing him, Elizabeth felt as if someone had poured a bucket of ice cubes down the back of her shirt. Alarmed, she bolted from the cubicle. Even if it was just a dream—and Elizabeth told herself that over and over again—she still couldn't bear to think that she'd come within an inch of kissing the man she hated most in the whole world.

Why? This question haunted her, refusing any simple answer. William White was *not* her fantasy. And there was no way she would ever kiss him, dead or alive.

Tears of frustration and fear sprang quickly to Elizabeth's eyes. Her throat felt tight, making it difficult for her to breathe. As she left the tent, Elizabeth was dimly aware of all the happy, excited faces swirling around her. *Why me?* she wondered, choking back a sob as she picked up her pace to get as far away from the crowds as possible.

Again the image of William's lips moving toward her filled Elizabeth's mind. It just didn't make sense. How could the man who stalked her and tried to kill her—not once, but *twice*—appear in both her CyberDreams disguised as her deepest fantasy?

Why not?

Elizabeth paused and took a deep breath. She couldn't deny it. Not completely. There was some strange, twisted part of her, deep down within her, that had wanted to see William White again. And that same part of her had wanted him to kiss her . . . and to kiss him back. Horrible as it now seemed and frightening though the CyberDreams had been, she knew that there had been moments where she had felt herself drawn to William, even found him attractive. It was as if the clock had been turned back. Back to a long-ago time when William had been so charming and persuasive that Elizabeth had even thought she might be in love with him.

And maybe I still am. . . .

No! Elizabeth told herself in horror.

Despite everything he did and everything he was, you can't deny you were drawn to him. . . .

Unconsciously Elizabeth put her hands up to her ears as if she could shut out her inner voice. The notion filled her with dread. But she couldn't ignore it. In a way, it was the only possible explanation that made any sense. The first CyberDream might simply have been a computer glitch, but two in a row? That kind of coincidence was too hard to swallow.

He's still in my subconscious. . . . Part of me must still love him. . . .

Yeah, right! Elizabeth shook her head. Maybe she'd cared for William once, but that was before he'd morphed into a complete psycho. Once William had shown his true colors, Elizabeth's feelings had shut off like a light switch. And nothing—*nothing*—could ever change that. No amount of smooth talking—not by Cyber-William, or by some nonexistent evil twin of his, or even by anyone who even remotely looked like or was related to him—could ever erase what William had done to her. Not to mention what he had done to everyone else.

William had terrorized the entire SVU campus, and although Elizabeth had never thought she could want anyone dead, she had felt only relief when William was buried and the whole saga was behind her. So why was his memory coming back to haunt her? Elizabeth had no idea.

Suddenly she felt goose bumps prickle the back of her arms. Someone was following her. Elizabeth didn't need to turn around to confirm it. Her instincts were positively screaming at her. There was someone behind her—and she had a pretty good idea who it was.

Just leave me alone! Elizabeth wanted to scream, but she couldn't manage more than a strangled sob. She felt trapped, helpless. He was chasing her in her mind—and now he was after her for real. Again. Back from the dead. And there would be no escape this time. There was only one thing she could do until the inevitable happened.

Run.

She broke into a jog. Tears of rage and frustration blurred her vision, but she pushed herself on. If William White was still alive, she knew she couldn't stop him from getting her. But she wasn't about to go to him willingly.

"Jonah! My man!" Bruce clapped Jonah on the back heartily. "You're just the guy I want to see!"

"Oh?" Jonah looked disinterested. His gaze lit

on Bruce for the briefest moment before it continued roving over the crowd outside the tent.

"Yeah! I was kind of hoping you might let me in for another quickie." Bruce's smile remained fixed and he tried to act relaxed, but inside he felt as if he'd just ridden a Jet Ski through a tsunami. Sure, Bruce remembered the rules—no one could have more than two CyberDreams. So what? Bruce was known for being a rule breaker. No laws could hold a man like him down. He just *had* to go again—nothing and no one was going to stop him. He was physically itching to get the headset back on.

"Sorry, Bruce. You've already gone twice." Jonah's tone was apologetic yet firm. "Rules are rules. And anyway, you can't go more than once a day, so even if you hadn't used up your quota, I'm afraid the answer would still be no."

"C'mon, Jonah. I'm a big boy." Bruce chuckled. "Look, I'm sure there's a good enough reason behind your rules and all—avoiding lawsuits, stuff like that. But you don't have to worry about me, man. I can handle another CyberDream. And"—he lowered his voice to a conspiratorial whisper—"it'll be just between you and me, bud. Bruce Patman is a man of his word."

"I'm sure you are, but . . . look. I don't care if you're five or if you're fifty. It's not healthy for anyone to exceed the limit," Jonah explained. "We can't be held responsible for how people might react. And we're not going to take that risk with you, OK? Not you, not anybody."

"Yeah, yeah, I can understand that. You're just doing your job. But I swear to you, I'm not going to go all wiggy or whatever 'cause of a third CyberDream. Just ignore the small print for once, dude! Come on!"

"Sorry. No can do."

Waving Jonah off, Bruce prepared to bring out the big guns. There was a brand-new fifty in his wallet just begging to see the light of day.

"Well . . ." Jonah sized up Bruce with his piercing, dark eyes. "Naturally there *is* a way to circumvent the rules," he admitted just as Bruce reached for his jacket pocket.

"Am I to assume we're on the same level here?" Bruce said, a smile creeping onto his face as Jonah nodded. Just as he suspected—the man had a price. Then again, didn't everyone? "OK, let's cut to the chase," Bruce said. Suddenly he was all business—cool, assured, and to the point. The language was money, and talk was cheap. Time to show the green and hit the tent.

"OK." Jonah turned away from the line and pulled Bruce over to the other side of the entrance. "The deal is one-fifty for the third dream, and you have to sign a waiver absolving us of all responsibility in case you have a bad trip."

"A hundred and fifty dollars?"

"You got it. Not a penny more, but not a

penny less either." Jonah leveled his gaze, appraising Bruce coolly.

Jeez, did I underestimate this guy, Bruce thought with admiration. Even though he could easily get the money, and even though he really wanted to take a third CyberDream, this was pushing it. Bruce didn't like throwing money away, and he certainly wasn't prepared to part with a hundred and fifty dollars of his hard-earned trust-fund allowance all for a few kicks. Plus Jonah wasn't exhibiting much in the way of salesmanship. He should have instantly offered a special gentleman's discount, not given Bruce the same option he gave to every other schmuck off the rack. Couldn't Jonah see that Bruce deserved better?

"No, thanks," Bruce responded dully. "I'm not that desperate." Jamming his hands into his pockets, he walked away, scowling. Part of him wanted to turn around and pay the guy whatever he asked. But Bruce's rational mind kept reminding him that the whole thing was totally ridiculous, not to mention the fact that Jonah's treatment of him was offensive. Yet he couldn't get the holotorch, the Patmachine, or Lila's red Lycra hot pants out of his mind. . . .

"Maybe I should go back," Bruce murmured. He could already envision himself back in the cubicle, sliding the headset over his ears, handing over three crisp fifties and giving in to that smug little—

"Nope. Not gonna do it. No way," he concluded. He'd be better off going back to Sigma house and playing Nintendo with his brothers. But with the white tent beckoning to him every time he crossed the quad, resisting the temptation to return was going to make for one wicked battle.

"Naw. I'm a man. I'll get over it," Bruce told himself firmly as he headed down University Avenue. "I can do without it. I think. . . ."

Elizabeth sobbed as a sharp pain ripped through her side. But she forced herself to go on. She could sense William's presence behind her, around her . . . everywhere.

The wind whistled past Elizabeth's ears, an eerie high-pitched wail like the cry of a child caught in a well. It swirled through her hair and stung her cheeks. Still Elizabeth pushed on, not knowing where she was going, but fully aware that the moment she stopped running was the moment *he* would get her!

As the wind moaned, Elizabeth began to realize that the sounds were gathering in force. And there was something else too—a human sound, like a low, sensual voice murmuring in her ear. He was there, his voice whispering and singing along with the gale.

Elizabeth . . . come to me!

"Never!" Elizabeth screamed, her throat raw.

Please . . . don't deny our love! William whispered,

his voice lilting, rising and falling in tune with the wind's pitch.

"Go back to your coffin!" Elizabeth yelled hoarsely, the pain at her side as excruciating as an open knife wound.

Let me love you. . . .

"No!" Elizabeth sobbed, stumbling as her toe hit a mound of grass.

I won't let you go, Elizabeth. I'll never let you go. . . .

"Stop!" Elizabeth lost her balance and fell into . . . something. Some*one!*

Sobbing in terror, she tightly closed her eyes, refusing to look at her tormentor. His arms coiled tightly around her, holding her in a grip as strong as a python's, taking her prisoner in the quad. *In real life.*

He wouldn't let her go. She was his now.

"Liz? Are you OK?"

With a gasp she stopped struggling. That voice—sweet, concerned, reassuring. Could it belong to . . .

"Tom?" Haltingly Elizabeth opened her eyes. At the sight of his kind, concerned face, she almost wept with relief. "Tom, oh, it's you!"

Elizabeth buried her head in the crook of Tom's neck, so grateful and exhausted, she thought she would faint. From the haven of Tom's arms she looked around the quad. William was nowhere to be seen. And his voice had disappeared too. She heard nothing but the rustle of leaves in the breeze and the murmur of Tom's loving words in her ear. She was safe. For now . . .

Jessica ducked behind Xavier Hall and took her compact out of her purse. Makeup—A-OK. Teeth—white and food free. "OK, just slink on past that tent one more time," she told herself as she checked the line of her bangs. "He checks you out, you go in for the kill." She shut her compact with a decisive click, stashed it away, and prepared to make her move.

With a toss of her hair Jessica crossed the quad and made another casual turn past the tent, nonchalantly glancing in Jonah's direction. Her plan was definitely yielding results. For the past half hour Jessica had been working Jonah like a pro, wandering by every so often and just when their eyes met, looking away. Now he was positively ogling her, and she meted out his reward—a longer, lustier look—as if he were a rottweiler slavering for treats. This was her method: holding his gaze for a fraction of a second more each time and then leaving him hanging. No way to treat a dog, but just the way to treat a guy.

But now she had to make her move before Jonah lost interest. It wouldn't be right for him to think she was just teasing him. Jonah was a babe, after all. Jessica was pretty sure she'd have to act quickly or risk losing him to someone far less attractive than she was.

She threw back her shoulders and sashayed up to the entrance. "Hey," she purred. "You'll never guess who costarred in my CyberDream."

"Who?" Jonah's eyes lit up with interest.

"You."

"Really? Must be my lucky day," Jonah murmured, his gaze riveted.

"Mmmm. Mine too," Jessica breathed. "My CyberDream was too wild, Jonah. It'd score an NC-seventeen easy." Well, maybe the fantasy hadn't been that supersexy on the surface, but it had made her feel R rated at the very least.

"You'll have to fill me in on the details." Jonah smiled, revealing a row of gorgeous teeth.

Jessica ran a hand through her hair and reveled in his gaze. "I'd be glad to fill you in, but you look kind of busy. I guess I'll just have to wait till you . . . get off."

Jonah averted his gaze toward a nearby cluster of shrubs. "Well, I don't know exactly when that'll be," he replied, his brow furrowing uncomfortably. Suddenly he turned to face her, his expression brightening. "Why don't you just hang here for now? We can talk, or . . . ?" he added, recovering some of his sexy charm.

Jessica bit her lip. "Or?"

"Nothing." With a James Dean pout he turned to stare at the ground. "Sorry. Forget I said that.

That was pretty stupid of me. I mean, this scene really isn't for you, right? You'd much rather go out dancing or something. . . ."

Aha—playing hard to get! He was totally ignoring her proposition and trying to make her play by his rules. She knew the technique well. *Obviously* he and Jessica were soul mates. She loved nothing more than a good challenge and, it seemed, the feeling was mutual. Jonah was quite possibly the perfect man. Or at the very least the perfect flirt.

As Jessica reflected on her next strategy, she couldn't ignore the bright neon signs flashing in her brain. They all read: Jonah Falk Is *the* One. Any man who could play her at her own game was a man to be reckoned with, especially if he had intense dark eyes and good taste in black clothing.

Now it's time for the hard sell, Jessica mused, switching gears. Simple class-A flirting wasn't going to cut it with Jonah anymore. He was practically begging her to grab the reins and pull.

"Well, anyone who works a full day has to take a break." Jessica raised her eyebrows ever so slightly. "You must get way tired standing there all day, talking to everyone. Don't you need to escape the crowd . . . just for a few minutes?"

Jonah grinned lazily. "I guess a few minutes couldn't hurt," he replied in a low voice. He grabbed a chain and hooked it across the tent's entrance. Hanging from the chain was a wooden sign reading Back in 10 Minutes. "OK. Come on."

Whoa! That was quick! Jessica thought, congratulating herself on her amazing ability to bend men's minds as she followed Jonah around to the back of the tent. Nearby greenery sheltered them both from passing students, professors, campus security, and the outside world in general.

"Just the two of us." Jessica wet her lips. "Whatever are we going to do?" She giggled, her eyes flashing mischievously. But Jonah didn't seem to hear. He was too busy looking around nervously as if he were afraid he might be spotted by someone.

"Don't worry—there's no way anyone can see us," Jessica cooed. "It's just you and me."

"Yeah . . . I know."

But Jonah kept glancing around as if he thought he were being watched. He was probably just afraid his supervisor or boss would pop up, Jessica reasoned. But why would he get so bent about it? It seemed hardly likely he'd get busted. Aside from Jonah she hadn't seen any other CyberDreams staff since the tent had appeared on the lawn. If there *was* a boss, he was keeping a pretty low profile.

All the more reason for you to relax, she told him silently as she moved closer to him. But Jonah barely seemed to remember that Jessica was there. He was way too busy fidgeting.

"Here. Let me loosen you up," she said, reaching up to massage his shoulders. He jumped at her touch. "What's the deal, Jonah?" Jessica demanded, feeling rejected.

"N-Nothing, sorry. Just too much coffee, that's all." Jonah slumped against the back of the tent and rubbed his eyes.

Well, kiss me and get it over with already, she commanded him mentally. But with each passing kissless second, excitement dwindled and irritation set in. Jonah's hotness meter plunged down to practically zero—and Jonah didn't seem to have a clue about it. No matter how many fiery glances Jessica aimed at him, he seemed too weirded out to return them. The two of them were well concealed enough to avoid making a public display. So what was his damage?

So he's got me alone with him and he won't even make a move? Jessica could think of hundreds of guys who'd kill to be in his position. In virtual reality Jonah was one of them, but now . . . what? Where was the sexy, flirtatious, lip-smacking Jonah she thought she knew? Had her CyberDream lied to her?

"So . . . how's everything going?" Jessica tried to keep her tone light, but she couldn't help the slight edge in her voice. At the very least he could admit he was unable to fraternize with clients or something. He owed her that much, didn't he? Whatever. She just needed *some* kind of explanation for his disappointing performance.

"Uh, nothing much." Jonah looked as awkward as a thirteen-year-old boy getting ready for his first kiss.

Uh, how about a D in Socializing 101? she mimicked in her mind. OK, this went far beyond playing hard to get. This was more like playing root canal. *Excruciating!* Why was Jonah making it so hard for Jessica to wrap him up and take him home?

Then an idea came to her. Maybe he was waiting for her to make the first move! It wasn't *exactly* her style, but things were getting boring, and if this was all part of Jonah's game plan, then Jessica was prepared to lose a few points and get what she came for—the kiss of her CyberDreams. If it took throwing herself at him, well, then that was just what she'd have to do.

A thrill leaped through her body as she slid her arms up around Jonah's neck and pulled his head down to hers. But as Jessica pressed her lips against Jonah's with every ounce of passion in her being, she didn't feel even a quarter of the sparks she had ignited in the Jonah of her CyberDream. It wasn't that Jonah didn't kiss back, but his kiss felt mechanical and clinical, as if he were responding out of duty rather than feeling. And Jessica could feel it.

What's with the wooden lips? Is this a chore?

As that thought ran through Jessica's mind, Jonah pulled away abruptly.

"Gotta get back to work." Jonah shrugged apologetically, but Jessica knew he was itching to get away.

Thanks a lot, loser, Jessica thought. *You really know how to make a girl feel special.* As they walked back around the tent, an awkward silence filled the space between them. Jessica had her nose as high up in the air as she could realistically manage without tripping. She felt a little cheap after the way Jonah had treated her, and although she refused to discuss it, it wouldn't hurt for him to see how miffed she was.

Jessica sulked a few paces behind Jonah. So much for fireworks—that kiss had scored about a two out of twenty on the lip-fest scale. How could he *not* have responded to her with unbridled lust? Guys just weren't like that with her. Well, not always. Sometimes they'd act all cautious and restrained, and still Jessica always saw it for what it was—an act.

Maybe Jonah was in some weird religious cult that outlawed kissing with feeling. Or maybe he was a robot. Maybe he had been pithed like a frog in biology class and his brain wasn't working quite right. Even then, there'd be no excuse.

Jessica's stomach twisted as Jonah said good-bye and headed back to work. But even though she was burning with resentment, she couldn't help feeling a twinge of sadness as he walked away.

Good-bye, man of my dreams, Jessica thought,

wincing as she realized how true her sentiments really were. The Jonah of her dreams had been so romantic, so bold and assured . . . *so* not *real!*

As she headed across the quad, she hoped that she was being too rash, too hasty. After all, the Jonah in her CyberDream had assigned the guy a reputation that would be hard to live up to. Maybe the real Jonah was just as passionate once he got warmed up. Yeah, that had to be it. Nothing else made sense. Obviously whatever was holding Jonah back had nothing to do with her.

OK, Jessica reasoned, *he deserves a second chance.* If it were any other guy, she'd drop him like a hot potato, but the Jonah of her CyberDreams was still too real in Jessica's mind to let go. As for the real Jonah Falk, Jessica could only hope he'd get caught up with his sexy alter ego sooner or later.

No, just sooner.

"Hop into my Porsche, baby—you're in for the ride of your life." Bruce gunned the engine and screeched away, burning rubber as he pulled onto the road leading to the beach.

"Hey! You could've waited until I was ready!" Lila snapped. "I almost got my new Chanel purse stuck in the car door."

"Speed is the key, baby." Bruce slid his seat forward and cranked up the stereo all in one deft flick of the remote control. As the car sped away, a surge of energy uplifted Bruce and wound him up all at the same time.

"What's with all the 'baby' stuff? You're talking like some cheesy guy from an old spy movie. The kind of guy who wears a toupee." Lila tossed her hair haughtily. "And you could try slowing down a little, OK? It's not like I've never been in your Porsche before. Your show-off days with me are over."

Bruce ignored Lila and concentrated instead on the buzz spreading through his insides and up his spine. He didn't know what had come over him, but he felt charged—crazy, almost. Like he could do anything and get away with it. His blue eyes glinted at the thought.

Totally wired—that's what Bruce was. He'd been wired and manic all day. Although he'd resisted the temptation to CyberDream a third time, he was by no means cured of the feeling his first two dreams had given him. Killing terrorists, overpowering snakes, screaming around hairpin bends in his Patmachine . . . it was all too tasty to forget.

Maybe he wasn't going to get the chance to be quite as wild in real life, but he was sure going to try and liven things up one way or another. He was wild and reckless, and nothing—especially not a whining girlfriend—could stop him from seeking out a killer thrill!

"Just hold on, baby," Bruce instructed Lila as they neared the beach. "I'm going to show you something."

"What?"

"The beach."

"The beach?" Lila snorted. "I've seen it, Bruce. It isn't exactly your invention, you know."

Bruce rolled his eyes. Man, was Lila being a pain. But not for long.

A smile spread across his face as he gunned the engine full throttle. *She's gonna love me for this!* he thought, picturing Lila's excitement when she saw what a daredevilish yet brilliantly executed stunt he was about to perform. She was whining now, but she'd be worshiping him in exactly two minutes.

"If you're going to drive so fast, then at least put the top up!" Lila screeched over the engine's roar. "You're killing my hair!"

"Your hair looks smashing, baby."

"Bruce, you *must* be joking."

"Me? *Never.*"

With that, Bruce cranked the Porsche into gear and sent it sailing off the drive and onto the sand. The car skidded and swerved until it eased out on the flat beach. Mmmm, sooo smooth.

"Bruce!"

"Check it out, baby! I give you . . . the sea!" Bruce revved and steered the car through the small waves breaking onto the sandbank. "Is this magic or what?" Bruce yelled as foam and spray hit the windshield. "Whoo-hoo!"

It was almost as good as a CyberDream. Almost.

"Bruce! Stop this—this—stupidity!" Lila yelled, putting up the passenger-side window as salt water sprayed her neck. The spray simply spattered over the window and into the car anyway. "You're totally soaking me!"

"The wet look becomes you, baby."

"Shut *up!* Jeez, when you said you were taking me for seafood, I thought we were going out to *dinner!*"

"C'mon, Li! A Saturday-night date doesn't get any better than this admit it!" Bruce hollered with excitement as he swerved to avoid a sizable wave. "Whoa, what a ride! What a rush!"

"This is not a rush, Bruce! It's a freaking bath! You've ruined my dress and you've *definitely* ruined my mood! Now get this thing onto the sand and let me out, *pronto!* I'm! Going! Home!"

Reluctantly Bruce steered the car onto dry sand. *Why are women such wusses?* he wondered, irritated. He'd pulled off a majorly cool stunt and all Lila could think about was her stupid dress and some lame, dull dinner!

"Listen, Rambo!" Lila yelled, her voice shaking as she opened her door. "I don't know what's got into you, but this macho display is not scoring any points with me. I'm cold, I'm hungry, and I'm *not* going to be treated this way!"

So much for being a Bond girl. Nope, Lila Fowler was a wimp! Bruce clenched his jaw in annoyance. Lila was supposed to be impressed by his amazing power and ravishing imagination, stunned by his reckless lust and rakish charm, and most of all, slain by his devastatingly romantic gesture. All he wanted to do was show her a seaside sunset with front-row, turbo-powered seating. Instead she was stalking off, clenching her purse like a housewife at a particularly annoying cocktail party.

As Bruce sat fuming in his car, he couldn't help feeling misunderstood and totally underappreciated. Lila was nothing but a spoiled sorority girl. She was nothing like the Lila of his CyberDreams. His virtual Lila would be up for more than just another night of champagne and oysters. She would live for the exciting, no-holds-barred dates Bruce had to offer. And she wouldn't just abandon him before the fun *really* got started. He was willing to bet a hundred and fifty bucks on that.

Chapter Eleven

"Don't worry, Liz. I'm here. You don't have to be scared."

Tom stroked Elizabeth's hand as she sat on her bed, looking skittishly around her. He felt just as nervous and terrified as she looked. He'd hoped that whatever had been making Elizabeth act so weird the day before had vanished overnight. At breakfast she'd been her lovable, chatty, upbeat self. But then when she'd literally crashed into him in the quad, running as if she were being pursued by a deranged killer, Tom knew that something was seriously up.

It had to be CyberDreams. Both of Elizabeth's hysterical attacks had occurred just after she'd dreamed. It was only common sense. But Elizabeth hadn't said anything about her second experience. And Tom was afraid to ask, afraid he'd get shouted down like the first time. Still, he figured it would be better for him to ask and get yelled at than get yelled at for not asking.

He studied Elizabeth's face, looking for clues. What could he do when she was behaving so unpredictably lately—swerving from anger to fear to cheerfulness? It was hard to know how to approach her. Maybe he'd just have to ask her straight up. Honesty was, after all, the basis of their relationship. Nothing would be achieved if they both kept avoiding the obvious issue.

"Liz," Tom began hesitantly. "You may not want to talk about it, but does this have something to do with your CyberDream?"

Elizabeth looked uncomfortable, but she nodded.

"Maybe it would help to tell me about it," he ventured, his voice low and soothing.

"I . . . can't." Elizabeth sighed, fidgeting with the sleeve of her sweater. She opened her mouth as if to speak, hesitated, then shut it again.

"Liz, you've got to open up to me." Tom tried not to sound impatient, but it was hard. "Tell me what you were going to say."

"I was just going to tell you that it . . . freaked me out. I don't really want to say more than that, though."

"Oh. Uh . . . OK."

"I'm sorry. I know I'm not being very clear right now; it's just that . . ." Elizabeth struggled for words, her eyes large and sorrowful. "It's just that the whole experience was really frightening for me, and I think it would be best if I didn't try to tell you about it right now. That would make it . . . too real," she finished quietly.

"But it wasn't real. That's the point."

"I know, but . . ." She clammed up and looked away.

So why won't you talk to me? Tom longed to ask. *Why won't you let me help you?* In the past Elizabeth rarely hesitated to confide in Tom whenever she had a problem, no matter how difficult. And he'd done the same. Tom was always ready to shoulder whatever burdens Elizabeth bore and lend a sympathetic ear, if nothing else. That was what he was there for. If she couldn't go to him with her fears, what did that say about them as a couple?

The thought seemed to open up an enormous canyon between the two of them. It was a depressing notion, to be sure, but what could Tom do to fix things? If Elizabeth wouldn't open up, he couldn't help her. Frustration welled up inside him, hot and sour.

"Please, Tom, don't be mad." Elizabeth's voice was pleading. "I just can't go back there, OK? Even if I just talk about it, I'll feel like I'm in that tent all over again."

"Fine," Tom replied in a low voice. He didn't even try to mask his feelings. *At least one of us is honest here,* he thought bitterly. There was only so much room for secrecy in their relationship.

Sighing, Tom ran a hand through his hair. A fleeting image of Princess Elizabeth's golden hair sprang to mind. A small, bittersweet smile flitted across his face as he thought of his princess waiting for him to rescue her.

What a contrast. And a welcome one too. Tom couldn't help it—he almost preferred the cyber-Elizabeth to the real one, even though he hadn't even so much as laid eyes on her face. Instinctively he knew that they'd be in sync. There would be no aching gulfs between them and certainly no secrets. Somehow—even though he knew it was all just a weird fantasy—Tom *believed in* the cyber-Elizabeth. And he knew no matter what conflicts they faced, they would always understand and support each other.

Right from the first CyberDream, Tom had gotten the feeling that they were spiritually connected. They hadn't even spoken, and still Tom could feel her right beside him every step of the way. And as the real Elizabeth lay on her bed right next to him, hiding all her thoughts and fears, she might as well have been on another planet.

He could hardly believe he was pining away after an image, a computer-generated fantasy. But it wasn't as if he didn't have a good reason. The reason was right in front of him—his girlfriend had turned into a stranger before his eyes.

Shaking his head, Tom tried to make sense of it

all. But it just didn't come together. How could Elizabeth *not* have a good CyberDream? They were supposed to be fun. He was sure every other student on campus was enjoying them. Everyone who walked out of that tent walked out smiling—everyone but Elizabeth, obviously.

And what was more, the CyberDreams were supposed to bring people closer to their innermost desires. It had sure worked for Tom. But Elizabeth? Well, she had literally run from her desires, kicking and screaming. Tom knew Elizabeth could get a little uptight sometimes, but this was ridiculous.

No, maybe it's just that simple, Tom reasoned. Elizabeth was just incapable of confronting and embracing who she really was inside. Maybe she simply couldn't handle being faced with her wildest dreams. Although Tom wasn't fond of that conclusion, it was the only one that made sense. And in that case, there was only one solution.

He gently stroked her arm. "You'd better stay away from CyberDreams, Liz. It obviously isn't for you."

And you're too closed off to accept who you really are, Tom added silently. He immediately bit his tongue and winced, wondering if Elizabeth could read his mind. There had been times when he had thought she could.

Obviously those times were gone because Elizabeth just nodded. "That's fine by me," she said. "Anyway, I don't exactly have a choice—and neither do you. We've both had our two tries. It's over."

Maybe for you, Tom thought. He couldn't even imagine leaving CyberDreams—and especially Princess Elizabeth—behind forever. He felt anxious at the mere idea. He wasn't about to acknowledge it, let alone accept it. That Jonah guy could threaten him all he liked with his bull about mental damage and whatever other scientific-sounding nonsense he could come up with. The only harm Tom could think of was in not ever seeing the face of his fantasy. If there really was something worth worrying about, he was willing to take the risk—a risk any knight could handle. He was going to meet Princess Elizabeth face-to-face, no matter the cost.

Lila stormed down the run-down, deserted ocean-side drive, resolutely ignoring Bruce's pleas from his beached Porsche. Why bother responding to such a boorish jerk?

She paused to wring water from her dripping wet, raw-silk Valentino shift. Anger and confusion boiled up inside her. She couldn't imagine what had gotten into Bruce. Sure, he acted like a five-year-old with startling regularity. And he never refrained from showing off in that dumb, frat-boy way of his. But as far as idiotic performances were concerned, this tumble through seawater took the prize.

And he's paying for it, Lila thought smugly. A delicious bolt of satisfaction leaped through her as she heard Bruce shouting and kicking his car in the distance. His reckless driving must have taken its toll on the Porsche—the engine was probably waterlogged. Now it wouldn't budge, and Lila was thrilled. Maybe he'd think twice before deciding to set his car on fire and plunge it off a cliff or whatever other moronic stunt was ticking away in that one-celled Patman brain.

Sometimes Lila simply could not figure out how men worked. *Must be all that testosterone,* she mused, shaking droplets from her hair. What other excuse was there? As for her, Lila had had more than enough excitement for the evening. The sooner she found a pay phone and a car service to take her back to campus and far away from the Amazing Bruce Patman Sideshow, the better.

Voilà! Lila spotted a pay phone and scrambled through her pocketbook for change. But before she'd even gotten to her coin purse, Lila spotted the loose coil of wire dangling from the end of the receiver. And the next phone she found proved to be just as useless. There was no dial tone. It was totally dead. And to top it off, the earpiece felt as if someone had spread honey all over it.

Well, there was nothing to do but wipe off her ear and keep walking. The night might as well go from bad to worse, right?

Lila headed away from the boulevard and down

a side street, aware that Bruce was jogging to catch up with her. *Let him run,* she thought angrily, picking up her pace. She wasn't waiting for that brainless wonder.

Shivering, her skin chafed raw from the combination of cold seawater and the force of the driving wind, Lila spotted an illuminated phone booth with relief—the only light on an otherwise dark street. She lifted the receiver and was thrilled to hear a dial tone. Thank goodness! Rescued by a pay phone.

"Hey!"

Lila screamed and whipped around. "Bruce!" She had nearly shot out of her skin with fear. She'd totally forgotten he was following her, and the sound of a voice on the quiet street had completely taken her by surprise. "You scared me—again!" she snapped. "Was that another one of your cool pranks for the evening?"

"I just wanted to see if you were OK," Bruce replied contritely.

"Well, as you can see, I'm not! But I *will* be just as soon as I get home and forget all about this lame excuse for a Saturday night."

"Come on," Bruce began, shrugging. "It wasn't a total disaster. After all, you've still got me . . . the world's most romantic man."

"Don't remind me!" Lila snapped. "I'm trying to get away from you, if you haven't figured that out. Now, if you really want to be good for something, give me change for the phone and green for the car. Then you can say good night."

Bruce's mouth opened and shut like a dying fish's. "Buh-Buh-But what about me?"

"You've done enough damage for one night, thank you very much," Lila retorted hotly. "I hardly feel like getting into that waterlogged beast, let alone riding home with you in it. Who knows? You'll probably jump into the front seat and take me for another 'romantic' seaside spin."

"Li—"

Lila held up a hand, cutting him off. "The money, Bruce. That's all I require right now. And it's the *least* you can do. After all, if I'd thought I'd be paying my own way back to campus, I would have brought more liquid cash!"

"Sure, Li. Anything you want." Bruce whipped out his wallet and began counting through a fistful of bills. "How much do you need? Fifteen? Twenty?"

"How should I know?" Lila yelled. "We're in the middle of Nowheresville and you expect me to know the price of carfare? What do I look like, a calculator?"

"No need to get huffy," Bruce replied indignantly. "You know, I'm trying to be reasonable about all of this. . . ."

"Reasonable?" Lila threw back her head and laughed. "You call this a *reasonable* situation? Honestly, Bruce, you need to get your head read."

Lila shivered as she felt a trickle of seawater run down the back of her leg and into her shoe. She could hardly believe her ears. Bruce Patman was no boyfriend. He was a joke.

"Let me just give you a fifty, then." Bruce pulled out a bill from his wallet and handed it to Lila.

"I think you'd better give that to us."

"Wha—?"

Before Lila could even finish her one available syllable, two greasy, scruffily dressed teenagers stepped out from behind a Dumpster.

"You heard us, lady," the guy with a red bandanna around his ankle said. "We want the money. Now hand it over."

Lila froze in terror as the other kid, a pimply guy with a mean-looking scar across his left cheek, grasped something in his jacket pocket. Something he aimed straight at Bruce's chest. The other guy did the same.

"Give it over now, buddy," Bandanna whispered, his voice low and menacing. "And give us all of it."

"Forget it, you scrawny creep," Bruce shot back.

"Give it to them," Lila urged. "This is not the time to be macho, Bruce."

"Your little girlfriend is right." Scarface sneered. "Of course, you have a choice, but it ain't a good one. It's your money or your life. And you've got three seconds to think it over."

Lila shut her eyes, hoping it was all just a dream. But it wasn't. It was real, and it was actually worse than anything else that had happened to her that night. Worse than getting splashed on. Worse than getting who knew what all over her ear.

Death in an alley—how *not* glamorous.

Elizabeth sighed and rolled onto her back. With Jessica snoring and the eerie whistling of the wind outside, she knew she was in for one long, agonizing, sleepless night.

Even if the room were perfectly still and quiet, she doubted she would have got much rest anyway. The events of the past two days kept replaying themselves over and over in her mind. Every time she tried to make sense of what had happened, contradictions fought a screaming match in her brain until she thought her head might burst.

Maybe I should count sheep, Elizabeth thought in desperation, but she knew she was too wound up to allow herself to focus on something so trivial.

And it wasn't only her mind that was racing. Ever since she'd left that awful CyberDreams tent, her pulse had been speeding and then slowing down in strange erratic bursts. And all because of William White.

Funny to think I once thought he was the perfect guy, Elizabeth mused, remembering how flattered she'd felt when William had first taken an interest in her. He'd seemed like such a catch—so different from all the other guys on campus. Aside from his dazzling good looks, William had seemed more mature and far more cultured than any of the other guys. And the way he'd shown his feelings to Elizabeth had really touched and impressed her. It wasn't just the flowers and old-fashioned poems, but also the romantic and elaborate dates.

William had once given her a magical evening at the ballet, and another time he had surprised her with tickets to the opera. What was more, he really seemed to enjoy both events and was amazingly knowledgeable about dance and music in general. Even if Tom took her to the opera, Elizabeth knew there was no way he'd really enjoy it.

She immediately chastised herself. How could she dare to even compare Tom to William? Maybe Tom wasn't all about Shakespearean sonnets and fancy cultural events, but he was hardly some bullish, uncultured jock. And more to the point, Tom was sane. Tom loved her. What about William?

William is psychotic, she reminded herself. *He doesn't love me. He never did. He's incapable of loving anyone but himself—*

Suddenly Elizabeth sat bolt upright in her bed. She could feel the color draining from her face. She'd been thinking of William in the present tense, as if he were alive!

She jumped. From out of nowhere came a

furtive, rhythmic scratching at her window.

Elizabeth felt as if she'd suddenly lost four pints of blood. She couldn't even move. She tried to will the sound away through sheer power of thought, but the scratching became even more insistent, as horrible to Elizabeth's ears as a nail file scraping against a chalkboard.

He is *alive,* she thought in horror, her hands gripping her comforter until her knuckles went white. William White was still alive. She could feel it in her bones—his evil presence drawing ever nearer. He'd come for her. Just as he had always promised.

"I'll love you forever. . . ."

As William's promise echoed in her mind and the scratching persisted, Elizabeth closed her eyes. *He's never going to let me go,* she realized, a dry sob catching at her throat.

Forever had begun. And unlike a nightmare, it would never end.

I should probably just hand it over, Bruce thought, sizing up the teens with a shrewd glance. It was the rational thing to do, and Bruce wouldn't exactly miss the cash. There was plenty more where that came from. But he was willing to bet anything that those "guns" pointing at him were just fingers.

"Bruce! Give them the money!" Lila squealed.

Bruce switched his gaze from Lila to the guys'

pockets. He was torn. He could be right about the guns . . . but then again, he could be very, very wrong. And if he was wrong, he probably wouldn't live long enough to realize it.

Still, Bruce wasn't ready to just give up the game like some kind of wimp pledge. No, this was the perfect opportunity to prove himself to Lila after a disastrous night. He knew he had a chance of beating the mangy mongrels and saving his money and his pride in the process. Lila wouldn't be so ready to spit fire at him once she saw how tough he really was.

A thrill raced through him. He knew what he had to do, and he was ready to do it. In a way this was the moment he'd been waiting for, the excitement he'd only cyberdreamed about. It was time to put his fantasy into action and confront danger head-on. He would let the tough guy inside of him out and send the creeps crying back into the gutter where they belonged.

"Not so fast, punk!" Bruce bellowed. He slammed his fist into one guy's belly, forcing his hand out of his jacket pocket. A wave of triumph washed over him as his suspicions were confirmed. No gun; nothing but a stubby, grimy little finger. A little finger he was about to snap like a pretzel stick.

Bruce was almost laughing out of sheer enjoyment as he grabbed the teen and slammed him against the wall. This was the rush he'd been waiting for. He was fighting the bad guys. *And winning!*

Suddenly Bruce felt a crack against his spine. The other guy had kicked him from behind.

"I'll . . . make . . . you . . . pay . . . for . . . that," Bruce choked out as he sank to his knees. But the second thug kicked him again, in the solar plexus this time. Before long the first guy had recovered and was pummeling at Bruce with surprising force.

"Ungghh," Bruce moaned as a fist connected with his mouth, sending a piece of tooth flying. After a last powerful punch in the eye, he became dimly aware of his wallet being lifted, Lila's wails, and the pattering of feet as the thieves fled the scene.

"Oh, Bruce!" Lila sobbed. "You should have just given them the money. You're such a *dope!*"

Bruce could only moan in response. Pain throbbed through his body. He felt as if he'd just been connected to a power plant and had fifty million volts pumped straight through him. Everything hurt, especially his mouth and his bruised right eye, which was already swollen by a lump the size of an egg. So much for being the big hero. First the Porsche, now him. The Patman and his Patmachine were both officially out of commission.

Groaning more from frustration than pain, Bruce smacked himself in the head for being such a jerk. Searing pain jolted through him. He'd momentarily forgotten about his bad eye and had hit himself square on his swollen flesh. For a moment he thought he would pass out.

"Oh, Bruce," Lila cried, her voice halting with nervous giggles. "Oh, you're such a mess. What a night, huh?"

Bruce swiped at the blood on his lip with his tongue. "Well, look on the bright side, Lila," he croaked. "You don't need that change for the phone now. Emergency calls are free."

Elizabeth grabbed the curtains and yanked them back to reveal . . . a tree branch. Elizabeth was so relieved, she felt positively weak. To look out that window and see only an innocent tree branch instead of two cold, ice blue eyes was like coming out of a dark tunnel and into the sunlight.

However, as Elizabeth slid her shaky legs back under the covers, she knew her battle wasn't even half over. He might not have come tonight, she reasoned, but that didn't mean he wasn't going to come tomorrow. Anything was possible. Nothing was certain. All Elizabeth knew was that somehow, William was out there. Bypassing all laws of logic and rationality, he was out there. And whether it was his ghost or whether he was still, somehow, inexplicably alive, William was haunting her. She knew it didn't make sense, but the fear she felt was very real. And all too familiar.

Elizabeth stared out at the eerily purple night sky. Hairline cracks of white lightning divided the darkness. There was no rain, but the wind still droned on, a strange, mournful howl. It was odd how closely the weather reflected her own tumultuous thoughts.

Perhaps it really is *all in my head,* she mused. Maybe when the weather cleared once and for all, she could put this episode behind her. She was just having some strange reaction to the weather, that's all. Maybe somehow the electrical storm had temporarily rewired her brain. It was far-fetched, but no more so than the idea that William White could still be alive.

But inside, Elizabeth knew she was grabbing at straws. The problem went far deeper than a couple of purple clouds and a forkful of lightning. William was there, pervading her every waking thought and experience. And at this rate she'd be an insomniac forever. Something had to be done. There had to be a way to lay to rest all the William White hallucinations, memories, manifestations, nightmares, or whatever they were once and for all. But how?

"Thank goodness you're all right, Bruce," Lila said breathlessly. "But honestly, I don't know what got into your head, trying to fight off those guys! Not one of your brightest ideas. And that's saying a *lot.*"

Lila helped Bruce into the cab and closed the door behind her, expelling a small sigh of relief as they sped away from the hospital. Finally the whole ordeal was behind them, although she still felt badly shaken up.

Bruce, on the other hand, didn't look anywhere near as shaken as Lila would have thought. Even though his eye was terribly swollen and his mouth all bruised and busted, he looked sullen rather than in pain.

And I know why, Lila mused, looking Bruce over knowingly. His ego had taken a much worse beating than his body had.

Of course Lila wasn't glad that Bruce had been so badly knocked around—especially since he'd been wearing the brand-new blue cashmere sweater she'd gotten him for his birthday—but she couldn't help feeling that the whole incident had happened to teach Bruce a lesson. He *wasn't* James Bond. He wasn't even Austin Powers. And it was high time he realized it.

It had been easy enough for Lila to put two and two together. This was all because of the CyberDreams. It didn't take a brain surgeon to figure out that Bruce had taken his fantasies a bit too far. Dreaming was one thing, but driving a Porsche into the sea and trying to fight off two muggers? Please! Dreams were dreams, and Bruce had just received a serious reality check.

"Swear to me you will not have another

CyberDream," Lila implored, fixing Bru vith her most pleading expression. "They're th ise of all this, you know. They've fried that pun le brain of yours."

"Pleashe," Bruce sputtered through a mo of cotton balls. Annoyed, he spat a wad of pi cotton into his hanky, and Lila looked away sq mishly. The whole scene was making her ill. on top of all the blood and guts, she still ha go home and face the fact that both her outfit Bruce's new sweater were completely ruined. N to mention the fact that Bruce's wallet was enemy hands. Thank goodness those creep weren't savvy enough to realize her Chanel purse was worth at least eight times more than whatever was floating around in Bruce's wallet. She clutched the purse and all the precious cosmetics nestled inside it to her chest, praying the nightmare was over.

"Bruce, you have to swear to me: no more CyberDreams. Swear it."

He pouted.

"Look, we already know that third sessions can be harmful, and I think we've had enough damage for one week, wouldn't you agree?"

"Hmmpph." Bruce acted as if he couldn't speak from pain, but Lila knew he was just stalling to avoid the issue. She was on to him, and she wasn't going to let go.

"Promise me, Bruce. Because if you don't, I'm

g to be even madder than I was when you ᵍd the waterproofing on your Porsche."

"OK," Bruce grunted, "but only if you make same promise. You've been pretty annoying er since you stepped into your shopping fantasy, nd I think another session might result in some erious damage to all credit cards within your each."

"Oh, so you *can* talk, huh," Lila replied evenly.

"Don't try and get out of it, Li. Remember, I just tried to pull the same stunt as you," Bruce added, wincing as he tried not to smile.

"Fine," Lila snapped. "It's a deal."

"Deal."

Lying through his teeth, Lila thought as she narrowed her eyes. She knew that shifty expression and that tone of voice. And she also knew she was doing the exact same thing. After a night of grim reality, she was only too ready to take one more step into cyberspace.

Chapter Twelve

He must be dead. Elizabeth was sure of it. She *knew* it—she'd seen William's lifeless eyes and his body slumped over the steering wheel. But still, she had to see him again, one more time, just in case by some remote chance he'd survived after all. The odds were next to impossible, but then again, William was no ordinary guy. . . .

Thick black smoke poured from the crumpled car and flames licked at its side like giant orange tongues. Elizabeth had leaped from the burning vehicle as soon as she'd found the strength to force open her car door. She'd had to cut her seat belt with the pocketknife on her key chain, but soon enough she had managed to get out, away from William's car and away from his frightening, dead eyes, a dull, deathly blue just like his lips.

Keep going! Elizabeth commanded herself as her shaky legs hesitated. She wanted to look into the car, but her body recoiled, instincts screaming at her to get away before the car exploded. She needed to take one more look. Just to make sure . . .

Elizabeth neared the car and stepped carefully toward the driver's side, her hands trembling. The window looked like a giant spiderweb, cracked into shards. It was difficult to see in, and she had to press her face against the glass.

The seat was empty.

Terror struck Elizabeth like the blow of a hammer, forcing her to jump back as she stumbled to make sense of what she *hadn't* seen.

Impossible! How could he have . . . ? Where did he—?

"Here."

Wheeling around sharply, Elizabeth looked straight into William's eyes. They were still as blank and dead as they had been in the car, yet there he was, right in front of her, smiling ghoulishly, a deep cut on the right side of his face dripping blood down the line of his shattered jaw.

As Elizabeth watched the blood course down William's sculpted cheekbones like red tears, she almost passed out from fear. But instead she could only stand there, watching in horror as William held out a white rosebud and took a step toward her. The rosebud was pale and creamy. It soon turned red, soaked with blood pouring from his injured hand.

"But you're dead!" Elizabeth sobbed as William slowly but steadily advanced. "You're dead!"

She put her hands up to her face as the bloody rose came closer and closer. Squeezing her eyes shut, she opened her mouth and howled, a loud, long, bloodcurdling scream. . . .

Where am I—yes. Thank goodness. Elizabeth sighed raggedly and lay back down on her pillows, listening to the sound of Jessica snoring away in the bed next to her. It had just been a nightmare. She'd had plenty of nightmares about William before. But this one had been awfully, incredibly vivid. Elizabeth was soaked in cold perspiration, her nightgown sticking uncomfortably to her skin.

Taking slow, deep breaths, Elizabeth forced herself to calm down. Oddly enough, it was Jessica's snoring that provided the most comfort. The fact that Jessica could sleep through anything—especially on a Sunday morning, when not even an earthquake could get her to open her eyes before twelve—made Elizabeth feel better. This was reality. Life was back to normal. She actually smiled when Jessica gave out a particularly loud snort. She never thought she'd be so happy to hear Jessica's snores. They were music to her ears.

Unfortunately the relief didn't have the long-lasting effect Elizabeth had hoped for. It didn't take long for the nightmarish images of William's pale face and bright red blood to come racing back in full, Technicolor detail.

But he died in that accident! Elizabeth reminded herself. She had been there. She had seen it. There was no way on earth he could have been faking, and there was no way on earth he could still be alive.

As she repeated this truth vehemently until it became a mantra, Elizabeth reduced the remnants of her terrifying dream to their bare essentials. The dream was nothing but a feeling of fear accompanied by a few creepy, yet seriously unrealistic possibilities. And it had no place in reality. Once Elizabeth felt sure of this, she managed to toss the dream out of her mind pretty successfully. It didn't really even scare her anymore, once she recognized it for the baloney it was. *Just my paranoia doing a number on my subconscious!* she thought, brightening as she felt peace of mind within reach.

As she got up and pulled on her robe, Elizabeth was seized with an idea. *Of course!* Suddenly it seemed surprising to her that she hadn't thought of it before. It was so simple, and it had been right in front of her nose all along. If she had managed to break down her fear by confronting her nightmare, then maybe she could take that method a step further.

It made perfect sense. William had been plaguing Elizabeth in her subconscious mind by terrifying her in her CyberDreams. And maybe if she took a stand and defied him, once and for all, she'd be free of her fear for good.

There it was. Her deepest desire. Her wildest dream. And it *would* come true. She'd make absolutely sure of it.

Elizabeth fixed herself coffee in the kitchenette and mulled over her idea once again. Obviously William was still haunting her deep down inside and the CyberDreams brought her fear to the surface. It was time to act and time, Elizabeth realized, for her conscious mind to stand up to her subconscious. There was no other way. If she didn't summon up the courage to face her fears, she'd be crippled, living under a black cloud for as long as her brain allowed it. And it was no good doing it from the outside. Elizabeth knew she had to get back into her CyberDream and do it from the inside. Like surgery for her soul.

This is it, Elizabeth thought, trembling partly from anxiety and partly from the triumph of the breakthrough at her fingertips. But there was one more obstacle to overcome: her fear of CyberDreams.

But you have no choice, she reminded herself. *You have to lay William to rest once and for all. To do that, you have to face him.*

Elizabeth looked out the window. She could see the tent from her room. The sight terrified her and at the same time filled her with guilt. Tom would never approve of what she was about to do.

But he'll never find out, Elizabeth thought. She

stared hard at the tent and then left the window to have her coffee and get dressed. She had places to go, CyberDreams to have, and the spirit of William White to exorcise.

A film of sweat coated Bruce's brow, the result of hours of agonizing decision making. He'd had a restless night. His brain practically turned itself inside out while his mouth and black eye throbbed. A painful symphony. After almost no sleep at all, Bruce had woken up groggy and jittery with an ear-splitting headache. What's more, neither painkillers nor strong coffee could cure him. There was only one thing that could.

Every cell in his body cried out for it, every fiber of his being screamed for the release of his pent-up frustrations and the soothing of his aching muscles. CyberDreams would take him away for one last, blissfully exhilarating ride. It would be the ride of a lifetime. Bruce could feel it in his blood.

But I promised Lila—and myself, Bruce recalled with a groan. He could hardly stand the pressure anymore. He'd thought he could make it through the day without succumbing to Jonah's bribe, but now, barely past noon, his resolve had crumbled. He just needed one more fix and then he'd be on top of the world. Just one last rush. It wasn't too much to ask for, was it?

Even if it only lasted a few minutes, Bruce knew a third CyberDream would take his mind off his painful injuries, messed-up car, and bruised ego. In CyberDreams he could be the *other* Bruce Patman—the one with the right moves, the right car, and the right woman. The decision was made.

Bruce made it to the CyberDreams tent in seconds and pulled Jonah aside to make the transaction. Already he felt his heartbeat accelerate in anticipation of the killer ride waiting just a few minutes away. He didn't even flinch as he handed Jonah the three fifties he'd taken from his emergency cash stash and signed the waiver without even reading it. His hands were shaking and his signature came out a crooked scrawl, but Bruce couldn't have cared less. His mind was on one thing and one thing only: He had to feed the monster, fill the need and feel the speed of a rushing, hard-core, high-stakes, big-thrills CyberDream.

And you're nearly there, buddy, he reassured himself, trembling as he waited for Jonah to issue him his ticket. He was hanging on for dear life. Relief was only seconds away.

"'By signing this document, you hereby waive your right to legally assign any damage to your mental, emotional, and/or physical health resulting from cyberdreaming more than twice in one lifetime to CyberDreams Incorporated, its employees, and/or its subsidiaries'—oh, puh-leeze!" Lila scoffed as she read the waiver. Utter garbage! She scribbled her signature and sailed into the tent without so much as a tremor. And once she had strapped her headset on and was ready to roll, she felt nothing but excitement.

The moment she was back in the arms of Virtual Bruce, she felt truly blissful. This was what she needed to put the moronic antics of Real Bruce behind her.

"Lila, you are the epitome of true femininity," Bruce murmured, stroking her hair as the limo hummed, gliding into the night with the smoothness of a luxury ocean-cruise liner. "With you, every second is perfect. I've never met anyone like you, Lila. You're as rare as the Hope diamond, and, I might add, far more lustrous and a million times more valuable."

"Why, Bruce, you say the sweetest things," Lila purred as he scooped a lump of caviar from a giant vat built into the seat. As he fed her the delicious morsels from a tiny gold spoon, Lila nibbled delicately, closing her eyes to savor the taste as well as the thrilling sensation of Bruce's lips nuzzling her neck.

Lila sighed as she dipped the spoon back into the caviar bowl and fed beluga to Bruce. She gazed raptly at the motions of his strong jaw as he chewed. He was such a delectable specimen of manhood—powerful yet gentle and as smooth, suave, and sophisticated as a man could ever be. *And he's mine—all mine!* Lila gloated, picturing the dozens of women who would weep and sell their mansions to be in her shoes for just one night.

"Kiss me, you angel," Bruce murmured. Without another word he pulled Lila into his arms, crushing her to his chest. As his lips met hers, Lila was astounded by the sheer force of Bruce's passion. As they kissed, his hands unpinning her elegant hairdo, her hands tracing his chiseled jaw, Lila felt as if she had been tossed over Niagara Falls. Waves of wondrous, dizzying, maddening love drove their kiss to a new height. It was primal—pure animal instinct at work—and Lila felt as if her entire body were on fire. She had been born for this moment—for this life. Now she could die happy!

"Wow . . . that was really something," Bruce declared when they finally broke apart for air. "This whole night has been extraordinary. You, Lila, were magnificent. Pity it has to end. Driver," he called out. "Stop here."

"Where are we?" Lila peered out of the window in confusion. All she could see were a maze of dark alleys, a couple of graffitied walls, and a ton of garbage cans spilling refuse onto the street. "Bruce, we must have made a wrong turn. This is nowhere near campus. We're in a totally skanky neighborhood!"

"Yeah, well . . ." Bruce chuckled and patted Lila's knee. "It's not my neighborhood, honey."

"What?" *Is he playing some kind of dumb joke?* Lila studied Bruce's expression for clues, but he still wore the same charming smile.

"Listen, Lila, I had a great time, babe. Like I said, they don't come any sexier than you. And I'll be sure to recommend you to all my friends."

"What? What's this about your friends? You know I hate your friends, Bruce! What's going on here?"

Bruce merely whipped out his billfold. "Fifty, one hundred . . . aaand a little extra for tip." He winked.

Lila thought she would faint from horror. *"Tip?"* she shrieked. "Bruce, are you on some kind of weird new medication?"

But Bruce didn't even seem to hear her. "See ya," he added, yawning disinterestedly as the driver opened the car door. "And thanks again. You're a real minx."

Minx? Lila's head was spinning. Why was Bruce treating her like this after they'd shared such a beautiful, romantic night with each other? And why was he leaving her in a sewer of a neighborhood with a fistful of cash?

The chips finally fell into place. Lila was no supermodel. And at that moment she felt a hole the size of a quarter burn its way through her stomach, growing and growing until she thought her insides were either going to melt or fall out of her completely.

Elizabeth slipped behind a pillar and looked furtively around the quad for Tom. When she was sure the coast was clear, she darted quickly to the far side of the quad. As the tent loomed before her, the white rosebud logo undulating as the wind whipped through the banner, Elizabeth couldn't help but feel a curious sense of excitement. No, not excitement—more like urgency.

But while Elizabeth tried to psych herself into what she thought was the appropriate, hard-edged, cold, fearless mode for her confrontation with William, she had to acknowledge an inkling of something else that had somehow managed to creep its way into her heart. She was anxious about seeing William, that was true. But it wasn't all about good-bye . . . or was it?

As Elizabeth slunk behind a tree, she tried to order the chaos inside her. Her mood swung from anger toward William to elation at the thought of seeing him again—his smooth, strong hands, his strikingly high cheekbones, his crystal eyes, which looked at her with such love and devotion. . . .

Stop!

Elizabeth shook her head to clear it of all thoughts and memories. Fixing her eyes on the ticket booth, she inched closer to the tent. It was time to end all of this, all the mixed-up feelings and crazy mood swings. It was time to get real.

Suddenly Elizabeth spotted someone else moving slowly in the distance, just out of the corner of her eye. *Tom!* He was hiding behind pillars and looking around him like a dog about to steal from the dinner table. And Elizabeth felt anger prickling at her skin like a million tiny needles.

Liar! she thought in disgust as she watched Tom slip into the tent. What a hypocrite! After the lecture Tom had given her about the danger of CyberDreams, Elizabeth thought it was a little rich to see him going back for more. All that time he was comforting her, he was probably secretly gearing up for round three!

She gritted her teeth, furious that Tom had not only had the gall to tell *her* what to do, but was blatantly ignoring his own righteous advice *and* purposefully trying to hide it from her too. That part hurt the most. Elizabeth hadn't expected Tom to be so downright underhanded.

Not that you *have a leg to stand on,* a guilty voice in her head reminded her. But Elizabeth knew her situation was totally different. She didn't want to cyberdream just for kicks. It was a matter of her sanity. Who knew, maybe her whole life was at stake.

And it wasn't as if she chose to go behind Tom's back. She didn't have a choice at all. In this catch-22, lying was the only option. Besides, Tom would never understand unless she told him about William. If she had done that, he'd have freaked out *and* sent her to the nearest psychiatrist to boot. And he certainly would never allow her to set foot in that tent again.

Anyway, Elizabeth reasoned, there was no

need to justify her actions, especially after Tom's flagrant lack of respect for honesty and integrity in their relationship. *I can do whatever I want,* Elizabeth thought, flouncing into the tent. *And if Tom says one thing and does another, then so can I.*

Elizabeth signed her waiver with a confident flourish. And after Jonah checked her signature and ID, he didn't even ask her to pay admission—her third trip was on the house, he said. Clearly she was doing the right thing. Everything was going her way.

She motored to her cubicle and put on her headset. All her confusing thoughts were as inconsequential as the static fizzing on the screen in front of her. She was giving Tom a taste of his own medicine *and* dealing with her past all at the same time. She couldn't have thought of a better way to spend a Sunday afternoon.

Of course, this had *nothing* to do with her wanting to see William again. Not in the least. She didn't feel even the teensiest thrill at the thought of seeing his handsome, achingly intense face and ice blue eyes gazing at her as if she were the most beautiful girl in the world. . . .

"Well, if it isn't Jessica Wakefield. What a *pleasant* surprise!"

Jessica groaned. Alison Quinn's clipped tones suggested anything but happiness at seeing her.

The prospect of making small talk with Miss Snippy was enough to make her long to have knitting needles stuck in her ears. But she was stuck with Stuck-up for at least ten minutes since Alison was directly behind her in line. There was no avoiding her least-favorite sorority sister. *Pity.* Jessica sighed, flashing Alison a quick, fake smile. She'd have to miss out on some prime pre-Jonah-fantasy fantasizing and cope with Alison's pathetic excuse for wit at the same time.

"So are you ready for your wildest adventure?" Alison trilled. "Let me guess, some little frat-boy love tryst?"

"Hardly." Jessica didn't even try to keep the edge out of her voice. "In fact," she added, "I don't really even need to go into the tent to have my wildest dream come true. He runs the show, if you know what I mean. . . ." She trailed off, dealing Alison a masterful Mona Lisa smile.

"No. I don't know what you mean." Alison sounded bothered, and Jessica was more than a little amused. Such was the lot of ugly ducklings who tried to ruffle swan feathers.

"We-ell," Jessica teased, keeping her tone light. "What I'm saying is that I don't really *need* the CyberDream. I'm already living out my fantasy, you know. He's right over there. I'm just playing the game until Jonah gets off work."

"Jonah!" Alison flushed, and Jessica could see jealousy tingeing her entire face a sickly shade of green. "Jonah Falk?" She pursed her thin lips together into a mean line.

Do we know any other Jonahs, doofus? Jessica smiled graciously and nodded. *Yes, lipless, I've already locked my plump pouters with the cyberstud . . . so dream on, sister!* Of course, as much as she would have loved to have said those very words, Jessica couldn't hurl such a flat insult at the Theta vice president. Still, a demure and slightly syrupy smile and an extra nod was a perfectly satisfactory alternative, and Jessica felt the kind of thrill that only a good snub could inspire. It was one of her favorite feelings in the world, and there was no one she would rather have shared it with than Alison Quinn.

"Funny," Alison retorted, recovering herself. "We seem to have the same taste—for once. I happen to have my eye on Jonah too." She smiled thinly and shrugged.

Alison's hot for Jonah? The thought would have been laughable if it wasn't so utterly hideous to contemplate. Not that Jessica had any fears about locking horns with stick-figure Alison over a god like Jonah. Obviously Alison didn't stand a chance.

Unless . . .

Rapidly Jessica's mind began whirling. Maybe Jonah was a bit of a womanizer. Maybe *that's* why he had acted so weird when they'd kissed. . . .

And maybe I have a very wild imagination,

Jessica reminded herself, tossing the thought out of her mind. She couldn't even bear to waste another moment's precious energy on such a wacko notion.

"Well, the fact of the matter is, I happen to have cyberdreamed about Jonah twice," Jessica explained. She couldn't very well tell Alison about her brief kiss with him behind the tent. It would sound tacky and besides, Alison had no right knowing her private business. "Jonah's been on my mind ever since we met, and I have to say, we've gotten pret-ty close in cyberspace, which proves it's all good." Jessica tossed her hair, wishing Jonah would appear and give her another meaningful glance to add some weight to what she was saying. But he was off behind a crowd of people who were signing waiver forms.

"Well, you're not the only one who cyberdreams about Mr. Virtual Reality," Alison retorted, her eyes flashing wickedly. "Jonah's been in both my dreams too, and the chemistry between us is *major.*"

What? Jessica's jaw dropped like a trapdoor, and she had to struggle in order to recover her composure. So much for each dream being tailored to fit the dreamer. The very idea of Alison and Jonah together—even if it was only in virtual reality—was ridiculous. They were hardly a match for each other.

It didn't take very long for Jessica to put

everything in perspective. Of course it was natural for a twit like Alison to dream of a hottie like Jonah, but that was all it was and all it could ever be—a fantasy.

No competition here, Jessica thought confidently. Alison could go right ahead and ride her idiot train into fool's paradise. She couldn't even cyberdream of touching Jessica in this competition. And since Jessica had the extra added comfort of being ahead of Alison in line—well, that meant Alison would just have to settle for second place in that department too. Jessica was up next, so she was getting to Jonah first.

Bruce screamed down a highway in the Patmachine, hot on the terrorists' trail. Lila's tracking necklace was doing the trick, leading Bruce right to the scene: inside the Patman Memorial Library on the SVU campus!

"I'm coming for you, honey bunny, so just sit tight! Bruce will save you!" Saying these words out loud helped psych him up for his next big obstacle—saving Lila and destroying the terrorists in one swift move. It would be no easy task, but Bruce was up for it. His heart beat loudly, and he felt adrenaline pumping through his veins like hot mercury. He was indestructible. And he knew how to destroy. Because when it came to saving his country and his woman, Bruce Patman was a killing machine.

Be afraid, suckers! Be very afraid! Bruce thought as he jumped out of the Patmachine and raced up to the main doors of the library, his toolbox of death in hand. He pushed and kicked at the door, but it was no use. It had been dead-bolted. That didn't stop Bruce from hearing Lila's frightened whimpers.

There was no other way in, Bruce knew. Heck, it was the Patman family library. Bruce had been there a trillion times. He didn't need a map to tell him the floor plan. *No worries,* Bruce told himself, glancing at his toolbox. He had a plan. He always had a plan.

"This is not over!" Bruce yelled. He opened the box and got to work, making plenty of noise so the terrorists would be sure to hear him. Bruce heard scuffling feet and terrified whispers inside the building and he smiled. They were freaking. And rightly so.

"OK!" he yelled, ripping sticks of supercompressed, multiple-density dynamite and electrical wires from the box. "You've got exactly five minutes to give yourselves up because if you don't, it's bye-bye, birdies!"

Bruce ripped a piece of duct tape with his teeth and secured the bomb to the door. "And don't think I won't do it!" he added, howling maniacally. "I don't care *who* you've got in there with you! It could be the queen of England for all the difference it makes to me! I just want to see you creeps die, and I'll make sure you do and enjoy every moment! *Yee-haw!*"

Roaring with laughter, Bruce pulled out every trick in the book in order to make himself sound completely insane. If the terrorists knew just how much he loved Lila, they'd know he had no intention of setting off any bomb. They'd know he would never jeopardize her life. But if he could convince them that he was just an everyday, average, garden-variety psycho killer, then he was in business.

A cunning smile spread across his face. A few threats and he'd flush them out faster than Liquid-Plumr. He was two steps ahead. Like always. This was going to be sweet!

Screeeech!

"Whoa!" Bruce's neck snapped like a whip. He'd turned just in time to see the terrorists making off in their van, tires burning on the parking-lot gravel.

No! He ran toward the van, but he was too late. How had they gotten out? Bruce immediately saw the answer—a window around the side of the library, the security bars bent and wrenched apart to create enough space for a man's body to slip through.

"Bruce!" Lila whimpered. "Help me! I can't get out!"

Oh no! The bomb! Bruce felt as though all his blood vessels had suddenly collapsed, leaving him light-headed and foggy. He rushed back to the front door, wincing with each scream coming from the other side. All he could see was the timer on the bomb, the seconds clocking down to zero. *Only two minutes left!*

"Don't worry, doll face, just sit tight!"

But Bruce had no idea how to disarm the bomb in the less than two minutes before it went off. And then . . . *Oh, duh! The window!*

"Li, climb out the window!" Bruce hollered. "It's right there!"

"I can't, you idiot! I'm all tied up!" Lila snapped. "Don't you think I would have done the obvious if I could have? Jeez, get some brains, moron!"

Oh no . . . Bruce's mouth turned dry with fear and his stomach began to churn queasily. There was no time to get into the window, free Lila, and get out again.

He had to disarm that bomb.

Cold sweat poured down Bruce's forehead as he gazed numbly at the counter.

Fifty-eight, fifty-seven, fifty-six . . .

The numbers glowed menacingly, and each second that passed hit Bruce like a punch to the gut. He was running out of time, and he had to save Lila. But he didn't have the faintest clue how.

Chapter Thirteen

"You really think they've hidden something away in here?" Jonah asked as Jessica led him across the train tracks at Redhill North.

"I heard 'em loud and clear," Jessica replied as they reached a barricaded entrance to the main building. "Hmmm . . ." She kicked at the door, but it wouldn't budge. "We need a different MO. Well, I guess if we can't get in the old-fashioned way . . ."

With an expert karate kick Jessica drove her right stiletto heel straight through the window-pane, sending shards of glass flying into the air.

"You never cease to amaze me," Jonah marveled.

Jessica shot him a sexy smile before hitching up her miniskirt and beckoning him over. "Give me a leg up," she commanded. "That way I can go in and unlock the door from the inside so you won't have to try and squeeze through that tiny window."

"Lucky you're so slim . . . and so smart!" Jonah cheered, cradling Jessica's foot in his strong hand as she slid as neatly and effortlessly through the window as a letter through a mail slot.

"Piece o' cake." Jessica lifted the bolt and opened the rusty door with a triumphant smile.

"There's no one around who can touch you, Wakefield." Jonah grinned and stroked Jessica's cheek, his eyes blazing passionately.

"Other than you, it seems," Jessica purred, relishing the sensation of Jonah's rough hand on her silky skin.

"*You* know what I mean."

"Of course. And . . . well, I'm glad you think so," Jessica began, "because I was just wondering what you thought of Alison Quinn."

"Alison?" Jonah frowned. "She's OK, I guess. Why are you asking me?"

"Just asking is all." Jessica flicked on her flashlight and began searching the train tracks, looking for suspicious objects or hidden crates. "Alison sure seems to like you," she continued airily.

Jonah put a hand on Jessica's arm. "Look at me," he commanded.

As Jessica looked into Jonah's piercing black eyes, a shiver of delight raced up her spine.

"I'm crazy about you, Jessica Wakefield. The Alisons of this world may come and go, but you're one of a kind—and you're the only girl for me." Jonah cupped Jessica's chin in his hand and brought his lips to hers, kissing her so forcefully that Jessica felt as if she'd just been shot with a stun gun.

"Oh, Jonah," she murmured, swooning from the headiness of his kiss. "You sure are improving."

"Very funny," Jonah muttered, the corners of his eyes crinkling with fake amusement. "And now that we've settled that, let's get back to work, shall we?"

"Roger-dodger."

Jessica was all business again, scouring the station with her expert eyes, shining her flashlight up pipes and into dark crevices. And then she saw it. It was so obvious that she'd barely even noticed it.

"The train car!" Jessica gestured at an old, dusty train car sitting to the side of the tracks on bricks, either waiting to be fixed or to be taken away.

As she and Jonah scrambled into the car, Jessica could feel that she was getting closer to her goal, inching ever nearer to the loot. And whatever it was, she knew that it would serve as the missing link—it was the clue that would tell her exactly why the mystery couple wanted Jonah dead.

Jessica swept her flashlight beam across the floor of the narrow carriage. It was empty, but something told her to keep going. And as the beam of light tracked across the walls, she spotted something. It wasn't very conspicuous—just the faint outline of a square in the faded, peeling wallpaper—but Jessica's superkeen detective's sixth sense told her she was on to something.

"This is interesting." Jessica ran her long nails over the square. "I think we may just have a secret panel here." She applied pressure to the bottom of the square and grinned as the panel swung out, the top half opening to reveal a small brown package taped to the underside. "Yes!" she exclaimed excitedly.

Jonah put a finger to his lips. "Did you hear that?" he whispered.

Jessica nodded. Voices from outside the train car. They were close—and getting closer. And although Jessica couldn't make out what they were saying, she still got the strangest feeling that she knew the speakers. However, now was not the time to find out. They had to get the package out of the car and hide!

"This way!" Jessica whispered, indicating the rear door of the car. The voices were coming from the other side, so Jessica knew they could get out if they hurried.

"Take this!" she added, tossing the mystery package to Jonah. It was heavy, and although Jessica was incredibly strong and agile, carrying unnecessary loads while she sought to make a dangerous getaway simply wasn't her style—especially when a male stood waiting to do her bidding.

Jonah caught the package just as Jessica heard footsteps directly outside the car.

Time to scram! Jessica turned to unlatch the rear door, feeling Jonah close behind her.

And then she heard it.

It sounded as if someone had just caught something that had been tossed by someone else. Something heavy.

The package?

Jessica stood rooted to the spot, trying to make sense of what she'd just heard. Warning bells clanged maddeningly in her head. Something was off. Something or . . . *someone!*

Wheeling around, Jessica stood face-to-face with Jonah. He was empty-handed.

"Are you setting me up?" she shrieked. There was no point in speaking in hushed tones now. Jessica saw confirmation of her worst fears in Jonah's eyes. He looked shifty and wouldn't reply.

"But . . ." Jessica was full of questions as she heard the couple moving through the car toward them. There was nothing to do but face them—face them all. She needed to see who Jonah was working with and why he had betrayed her.

A man loomed behind Jonah, and Jessica could see that he held the package in his hands. Angrily she shone her flashlight in his face. And then she did a double take, nearly fainting from fright. Jonah stood next to . . . *Jonah?*

The two men were mirror images of each other—more identical than Jessica and Elizabeth, from their thick dark eyebrows and the tiny moles on their left cheeks to the clothes they were wearing. Jessica blinked, but the same two faces stared back at her no matter how many times she closed and opened her eyes.

"Hey, Jessica . . . what's wrong?" her Jonah asked. "Why are you looking at me like that?"

"*Excuse* me? Because there's *two* of you, *duh!*"

"Not for long!" the other woman shouted. "There's only *one* Jonah Falk . . . and he's *all mine.*"

The woman stepped into the light, but Jessica looked away, shuddering in disgust. She didn't need to look at her competitor to know she was *Alison Quinn.*

Champagne and only one glass? Doesn't seem like your style, William. . . .

Elizabeth studied the rest of the objects on display before her. She was seated on a red-and-white-checkered blanket, a bucket of champagne on ice in front of her as well as a bunch of grapes.

Maybe this is it, she thought, confused. *Maybe it is just me in this dream.* Everything was back to normal now, and her wildest fantasy was simply for her to be alone and relaxed. After everything she'd been through, a nice picnic in the sun all by herself could easily be the perfect CyberDream.

But as she took in her surroundings, Elizabeth realized her hopes for being alone were probably nothing more than wishful thinking. She was seated on the edge of a high cliff. The sea curled gently toward the windswept beach below, and the landscape was beautiful. But just one quick peek over the edge gave Elizabeth the creeps. Suddenly she felt about as secure as a wind chime in a hailstorm. From the vertiginous view to the grass rustling like a million snakes, the atmosphere was charged with a strong sense of foreboding. And Elizabeth had a pretty good idea why.

"William, I know you're here. You might as well show your face." Elizabeth tried to sound strong, but to her own ears her voice seemed tinny and small. "William?" Elizabeth glanced fearfully around her. Still nothing—nothing but the rushing wind and the distant roar of the sea.

This is silly! Elizabeth told herself. *If he* is *here, why hasn't he shown his face yet?* Maybe William was waiting to surprise her. Or maybe he was waiting for her to find him. Or maybe there was no one there at all and she was simply losing her mind.

Elizabeth sighed and stared at her champagne glass. She hoped the picnic really *was* nothing but an innocent dream. Her deepest wish was to sit by herself, looking at a beautiful beach and toasting the end of her nightmares. There was nothing to do but wait to see what—if anything—materialized.

While she waited, Elizabeth sipped the champagne. So deliciously bubbly and refreshing. It made her feel bold, light-headed. She knew then that if William White did decide to make an appearance, she would stand up to him. She would show him how fearless and brave she really was.

As if to prove herself, she drained her glass and stood up to take a step toward the cliff's edge. She was ready to face her fears and overcome them. She forced her eyes downward to stare at her feet. Shifting her gaze slightly, she focused on the beach laid out below her, a long, sheer drop down. . . .

Suddenly the ground lurched beneath her feet. Elizabeth looked up in a panic. The horizon teetered from side to side like a seesaw. Stumbling backward, she slipped—and landed firmly on the picnic blanket. The ground stopped swaying and she closed her eyes. Safe. She was anchored to the ground, safe on terra firma—

"Perhaps you drank a little too much, too fast."

Elizabeth gasped.

"Champagne should be savored, not swigged, you know."

Her eyelids flew open and she struggled to sit up. He was there with her, casually dressed in jeans and a white T-shirt. Seated, sharing the blanket, smiling at her affectionately.

As she turned away, Elizabeth felt something soft graze the side of her cheek. The silken petals of a white rosebud. Surprisingly, Elizabeth felt very little fear. Maybe it was the champagne, maybe the accumulation of William's tauntings—whatever it was, at that moment she felt confident and rooted, ready for anything.

"Glad to see you, William." Elizabeth's voice was cold but sincere. She *was* glad he showed up. She was supposed to face the music. She was supposed to tell him to get out of her head and out of her life forever.

Wasn't she?

That was why she was glad to see him . . . right?

"Strawberry?" William dangled a huge, ripe strawberry in the air. It swayed back and forth imperceptively.

Elizabeth blinked, frowning in confusion. Where did that come from? She had been sitting on that blanket for who knew how long, but she couldn't recall ever seeing strawberries . . . or cherries . . . or chocolate mousse . . . or hazelnut ice cream. . . . In that brief moment when she'd turned her back on the spread, not only had William appeared from nowhere, but he'd also somehow managed to transform her simple picnic into a gourmet event for two. There was even an extra champagne glass and a fresh bottle cooling in the ice bucket. White rosebuds had been scattered everywhere.

"Very impressive, William," Elizabeth remarked. "But you aren't quite getting it, are you? I don't want this. Any of it. And I don't want you."

"Are you sure about that?" William's eyes were all passion now and he gazed at Elizabeth full force, hiding nothing of his intensity.

Elizabeth felt a little woozy as she struggled to tear her gaze away from William's. *It's just the champagne,* she told herself. He didn't have a hold on her. She could still be strong. . . .

"Oh, Elizabeth." William sighed huskily as he sifted his hands through the piles of soft, white rosebuds strewn around him. "Can't you see how much I love you? Can't you feel it?"

"N-No," Elizabeth stammered. Her head was beginning to throb from the effects of the champagne combined with the sweet, heady perfume of the rose petals.

"All this"—William gestured at the flowers and food—"I did this for you. Because I want you. Because I love you." He poured champagne into his glass and took a small sip, his eyes shining. "Perhaps I sound a little trite, repeating those words that so many have used insincerely. Still, what other words do I have to adequately express my feelings? I love you, Elizabeth." He paused, fixing Elizabeth with a gaze full of adoration. "But you know that."

"N-No—"

"Oh yes." William's voice was firm and low. "All of this. And more. It's all for you. And only I can give it to you—"

"No. It's just m—*your* . . . sick . . . fantasy," Elizabeth spat out. "You don't love me. You never did. You're . . . possessive. And selfish. And egomaniacal." Elizabeth turned fully away from William. She couldn't stop herself from looking at him otherwise. And looking at him only made her feel confused; hypnotized, even. She needed to keep her head clear. She couldn't let him get inside it any more than he already was. She needed to block him out of her mind and out of her life forever.

Just hold on, she coached herself, but still she couldn't quite keep herself from looking at William one more time. He had sounded so sincere, so loving. And his eyes burned into hers with a strength that threatened to melt her resolve. How could anyone who hated the world look so beautiful? How could anyone so murderous still gaze with his eyes full of love?

Maybe I'm *the one full of hatred,* Elizabeth thought, slipping into uncertainty all over again. *Maybe* I'm *the murderous one.* After all, she *had* wanted a showdown with him. She *had* thought that killing him in her dream would rid him from her mind and her life forever.

How could she have thought that way? Now that he was sitting there, right next to her, she couldn't imagine actually doing anything to hurt him . . . even if it *was* all in her mind.

And once Elizabeth allowed herself to look at

William again, his eyes never once wavered from hers.

"Everything I've ever done, I've done for you, Elizabeth," he said with confidence and clarity.

Look away, Elizabeth commanded herself, but she couldn't. She was slipping, falling under William's spell. Again.

"For you," William repeated. "For you. Always for you . . ."

As Tom slipped on his headset, he felt as if he'd just returned home after a long and horrible train journey. The fee had been awfully steep, but Tom hadn't even hesitated to dip into his trust fund and pay up. He was willing to give up anything to get back to the tower—and to the Elizabeth of his dreams. And there she stood right now before him, spinning at her spinning wheel.

Tom sighed. Hanging with Princess Elizabeth would *definitely* prove to be more exciting and romantic than being with the real Elizabeth, he knew. That woman was just no fun these days. What guy *wouldn't* get tired of having a girlfriend who was either freaking out or closing herself off from him every other minute? Princess Elizabeth would never shut him out, and she'd never have a *single* irrational conniption fit, let alone several a day. No spaz attacks, no secrets. She would share everything with him, he'd share everything with her, and they'd live *happily ever after.* All he needed to do now was to get her out of this big old tower and onto his stallion. Then they'd ride off into the sunset for a slightly hotter-than-fairy-tale romance.

Tom rushed over to the spinning wheel. Quick as a flash Elizabeth bolted away, slipping through a side door.

"Don't be afraid!" Tom called out. The poor girl—she'd obviously been through too much to trust anyone. No wonder she wouldn't even look at him, let alone answer.

His heart clenched with pity at the thought. Princess Elizabeth really needed him, obviously. He'd soon show her that he was her knight in shining armor. Yes, he was going to take her away from all this hiding away in caves and imprisonment in towers and spinning at spinning wheels nonsense. He'd take care of her and protect her forever, no matter what.

But before Tom could make good on any of his noble proclamations, he had to get off his can and find that elusive princess all over again.

This place is a maze, Tom reflected as he wandered through narrow tunnel after narrow tunnel. The princess had disappeared so quickly, he hadn't been able to see which path she had taken. The odds of finding her were firmly stacked against him.

"But I shall find thee!" Tom declared. He could kill dragons and slay witches easily. How hard could it be to find a girl in a tower?

For minutes on minutes Tom raced through the tunnels. He rounded the corner of yet another dark tunnel, bending over to keep from hitting his head on the low ceiling. A shadow leaped on the far wall, lit by a flickering tallow candle swinging from a small metal lamp.

Maybe she's down there! Tom's heart skipped a beat as he headed in the direction of the shadow. He took care not to make too much noise; he didn't want to frighten her. If she heard him so much as breathe, she'd bolt. His only course of action was to sneak up on her. She would be startled, to be sure, but at least they would meet face-to-face and she could see that her pursuer was, in fact, her rescuer.

Yes! She's here! Tom hid behind a crumbling wall, positioning his eye at a keyhole-size gap where the bricks didn't quite meet. It was the perfect vantage point from which to see the princess and yet not be seen by her.

But what he had found was anything *but* the beautiful Princess Elizabeth. Instead Tom found himself looking straight into the glowing red eyes of a huge bat. As it flapped its giant wings, Tom barely moved a muscle. Bats were highly sensitive creatures, and this was no ordinary bat. Tom's eyes practically bulged out of their sockets as he took in the bat's giant capelike wings and shiny fangs. The creature looked a bit too much like

Dracula for Tom's liking. And clearly it had a lust for blood from the way it sniffed the air and cast its beady eyes around the room.

"Avast," Tom declared as he fingered a tiny but razor-sharp ruby-encrusted dagger on his belt. "I must dispose of thee before thou disposest of me!"

With a quick, expert throw of his dagger Tom caught the creature right between the eyes. It gave out a last, shrill squeak, beat its wings feebly, and dropped to the floor, where it lay quaking for a moment before finally going still.

Nice house pet, witch, Tom thought as he went over to study the bat. As dead as a doornail! Satisfied with his handiwork but annoyed at the delay, Tom pulled his dagger out of the bat's giant head and moved on.

The next tunnel was equally long and gloomy, and Tom was beginning to give up hope. From the looks of things, there was literally a labyrinth of possibilities for Elizabeth to hide in. But suddenly there came the signs: a patter of feet and a flash of golden hair lighting up the darkness before disappearing from view.

"Princess, please! I will not hurt thee!" Tom called out, sprinting to the end of the tunnel. He felt frustrated by the silence that greeted his cry, but he hadn't really expected otherwise. The princess was just afraid, that was all. She would come to him willingly in the end. He could practically feel it—it was as if her spirit were calling to him while her body tried to flee.

I bet she isn't quite ready for me, Tom thought, a small smile on his lips as he pictured the timid look he would find on his sweetheart's face. He had no choice but to keep chasing her until he caught her. And once he held her in his arms, all her resistance would melt away. They would be joined together at last. And they'd never let each other go. . . .

Tom frowned when he reached the foot of a spiral staircase. Looking up, he noted that it seemed to end in midair. But as he climbed, he spotted a dark hole in the wall from out of the corner of his eye. It was the only path away from the staircase. *She's leading me to her,* he realized, suddenly jubilant. *She wants to escape, but she wants me to follow. And follow I shall!*

Tom slid into the dark hole and crawled, wondering where he was going. And then he saw a shape—large, round, familiar, but distinctly not human: A rat stood blocking his path.

Is he on growth hormones? Tom wondered, amazed and appalled at the giant beast, whiskers quivering, eyes gleaming evilly. The creature glared at him and bared two neat rows of sharp teeth. It sat back on its haunches, ready to pounce. The rat looked enormous enough to have a human appetite.

An appetite for humans, that is, Tom thought

with a nervous gulp as he spotted a bleached skull lying to the left of the rat. Well, this rat wasn't about to get a taste of Tom Watts anytime soon. Lying down wasn't exactly the greatest vantage position for beast slaying, but Tom still managed to slide a hand over to his dagger just as the rat leaped into the air. Tom held the dagger level with his neck, catching the rat in the throat like a chunk of meat on a shish kebab skewer.

Tom closed his eyes as the rat's blood spurted, but the shower was over soon enough. The creature lay still, and Tom gingerly replaced his sticky blade on his belt. Killing the rat *had* been a necessary—although rather gross—move, except that it yielded one problem: The rat now blocked up the rest of the tunnel. And like in any traffic problem where something blocked the route, Tom couldn't see how to bypass the obstruction without moving back the way he came.

But then I'll never find her! Tom realized forlornly. However, he had no choice.

Tom crawled dejectedly out of the tunnel and back to the spiral staircase. And then he saw it—a flash of blond hair at the bottom of the stairs.

"No! Wait!" Tom cried as the princess darted away, obviously surprised by his sudden reappearance. Elizabeth didn't stop at Tom's words, nor did he. He was determined to rescue her even if she didn't know it. He was gaining on her. Just a few more strides and she'd be in his arms.

Done! Tom's arms enfolded the princess's slender frame from behind and he felt her stiffen in his embrace. *Not for long,* he thought happily. *Once she looks into my eyes, she'll see only love. . . .*

After all the dangerous obstacles and an exhausting chase, Tom finally had his arms around the woman he loved. And after all this time he would get to see her beautiful heart-shaped face instead of just the curtain of long, golden hair falling down her back.

Gently Sir Tom turned Princess Elizabeth around in his arms, his heart pounding with the thrill of the revelation to come.

Just stand your ground, Elizabeth told herself as William's words of love flowed as smoothly as water over pebbles. She *had* to keep telling him no. She had to. . . .

But William wasn't even slightly deterred by Elizabeth's protestations. If anything, it only made him try harder. "If you would only allow yourself to believe me, you'll find what I say is true," William continued, pleading with his eyes, his voice deep and sonorous.

"No. None of what you're saying is true, and none of this is real. You're just a bad dream and—and I want you to get out of my head."

"Oh, Elizabeth." William's voice broke. "I know you're fighting me, but I love you too much to let you go. From the moment I first saw you, I knew you were my future just as I knew I would be yours—"

"No!" Elizabeth shouted, but William wouldn't stop. Declaring his love with poetic flair, he continued, never once fumbling for words, his voice assured and sincere.

"Please stop," Elizabeth begged, her voice faltering as William described the depth of his feelings and promised undying love, his face achingly beautiful in the clear, crisp light. It was so hard to keep resisting, especially when he wouldn't take no for an answer. But she had to resist. If she wasn't firm with him, she'd never be free. And she wanted desperately to be free from him . . . didn't she?

"No," Elizabeth repeated. "I—I don't love you, William. And we will never be together. Never."

"Please don't . . ." William winced as if Elizabeth's words were stones hitting his body. "It hurts. . . ."

Elizabeth stood up and backed away from William, unable to bear the sight of his gorgeous, magnetic face or listen to his soothing, mesmerizing voice. As William stood up to walk toward her, she felt helpless and caught. But she had to get away from him. It was the only answer . . . but she had nowhere to go.

Nowhere but down, Elizabeth realized as she found herself standing almost at the edge of the cliff.

Chapter Fourteen

"There *must* be a way to shut this thing off," Bruce murmured. He tried to calm down and concentrate on defusing the bomb he'd somehow slapped together, but Lila's screams from inside the library tore his insides to pieces.

Less than a minute to go! he realized in horror as the red digital numbers ticked away, a countdown to certain, sudden death. . . .

"Don't even think that!" Bruce berated himself.

"*What*, Bruce?" Lila screamed. "Oh, great! Are you *talking* to yourself now?"

"Uh . . . don't worry, sweetheart!" he bellowed, forcing himself to sound confident. "I've got it covered! We're going to get you out of there in just a few more seconds!"

His palms sweating, Bruce tried to sort through the complicated wires of the fuse box, but he had no idea what he was doing. *Think,*

Patman, think! he commanded himself, but all he could do was stare at the rapidly descending numbers. There had to be a solution, he knew. But even with Lila's life on the line, Bruce couldn't come up with a single thing. His head was a void, his skin icy and boiling hot all at the same time.

"Bruce?" Lila wailed. "Bruce, please save me!"

"I will. Don't worry, Li." But Bruce's voice was hoarse with tears that he was fighting to control. She couldn't know what was about to come. Bruce had to keep the truth from her. It was the least he could do.

Twelve . . . eleven . . . ten . . .

The numbers were mesmerizing, each like a knife to Bruce's heart. There was nothing left to do but give up and run away. This was one battle he was not going to win.

Seven . . . six . . . five . . .

"Bruce?" Lila whispered, her voice quavering. "Am I going to die?"

"No, baby." Bruce fought to keep his voice controlled. "I love you," he added softly, knowing those would be the last words she'd ever hear. And then, turning away, Bruce bolted, diving onto the grass lawn next to the parking lot.

Two . . . one . . .

Bruce prayed for a miracle, prayed that somehow he'd wired the bomb all wrong, prayed it wouldn't go off.

Boooooom!

Bruce felt a searing heat engulf him, and he rolled as far away as he could. Through eyes bleary with tears, he turned his head and looked at the sight he knew would forever be emblazoned on his memory. The library was a pile of flaming rubble.

"Please, Li," he begged irrationally, salt stinging his cheeks. "Just walk out of there now. Just tell me everything's going to be OK."

But she didn't.

Lila was gone.

And it was all his fault.

Bruce stood up and looked at the blazing inferno, distorted through his tears. "Good-bye, Lila," he croaked. "I'll always love you. And I'll never forgive myself. . . ." He trailed off as the smoke and flames dissolved into static. He stood dumbfounded for a long moment before he removed his headset with shaking hands.

"That . . . sucked!" Bruce choked out. His throat was constricted, and he felt nauseous. All he wanted to do was get out of that tent and run away. Away from those stupid machines and the vivid nightmare they had created. "That's it, man. I'm done with this game. That was really, really *sick*."

"Just leave me!" Elizabeth yelled, her voice filled with hysteria. But William kept moving toward her, his steps slow and steady.

"Come back here, Elizabeth," he coaxed. "That's enough hysterics now, don't you think?"

William's calm, patronizing voice only enraged Elizabeth, and she was seized with loathing, a loathing so strong that it fueled her to keep moving backward. Even though she was perilously close to the edge of the cliff, anything was preferable to moving toward William, and every step he took toward her made her step back instinctively. They were poles of magnetic force, and their movement was beyond Elizabeth's control.

"Now, don't be silly," William chided. "It's time you stopped lying to yourself and running away from me. I love you, and you *will* accept that."

Elizabeth watched his gaze carefully. His eyes were steely with an anger William was clearly trying not to show. He was near the end of his rope. *He's going to lose his temper,* she realized fearfully. *And we all know what happens then.*

How could she ever have let him lull her into thinking he was her fantasy, even for a second? The idea was about as insane as William himself was—and she was *not* going to let him get her. Not this time. *It's* my *dream,* she reminded herself. I'm *in charge of this thing, not William White!*

"Get away from me!" Elizabeth cried, glaring at William as if he were dirt.

"Never," he whispered. "I'd rather die than let you go. Or"—he cocked his head to one side, a small, deranged smile twitching at the corners of his lips—"you can have it the other way around if you'd like." He held his hands in front of him and made pushing gestures. "Your choice."

"No!" Elizabeth took off and ran along the edge of the cliff, struggling to keep her eyes away from the sheer drop to her left while trying to focus on placing her feet securely. One false move and she would be dead.

But there's no other way, Elizabeth thought, stifling a sob as she heard William's steady footsteps behind her. If she darted out to the side, he'd catch her. But if she kept to the spine of the cliff, he could only follow her or else risk his own life tackling her to the ground. And no matter what William said, Elizabeth knew he'd never go that far.

He'd kill me, Elizabeth thought as tears sprang to her eyes, *but he'll make sure he gets away alive. He always does. . . .*

William chuckled behind her, his laughter warped by the wind. The sinister sound spurred Elizabeth to run faster, but she was on a tightrope with death waiting on either side.

Don't look down! Elizabeth commanded herself, butterflies of panic fluttering inside her stomach, her palms clammy from fear. *Don't look back!*

Yet she knew he was gaining on her. She could practically feel his breath on her neck.

"Elizabeth!" William cried. "You can't run and you can't hide!" As he howled with laughter, Elizabeth's vision suddenly went blurry with tears. Her foot caught on a pebble and she felt herself slide, saw the hard ground, heard William's words echo through her mind, and watched the flat, blue sea below reach up to her.

I don't want to die like this!

With a desperate yelp Elizabeth felt her feet slipping from ground into air. She grasped for anything firm, clutched for the ground. And everything stopped just as quickly as it had begun.

Disoriented, Elizabeth wondered if she were dead. Then she opened her eyes and looked around her.

She screamed and sobbed. Dangling on the edge of the cliff, there was nothing but a few roots clutched in her right hand that separated her from life and death.

"Elizabeth!"

Looking up through her tears, she saw William, holding out his hand. Not a trace of laughter on his face. "Take it."

Elizabeth stared into William's eyes. This was just a dream, she knew. Just a fantasy. It wasn't real. If she just let go and fell, would she come out of her CyberDream OK?

She thought back to the last two CyberDreams she'd had. She'd nearly lost herself both times. And then she remembered that old wives' tale. What was it again? Oh yeah. *If you fall in your dreams and don't wake up before you hit the ground, you die in real life.*

You die. . . .

Elizabeth gulped. Something told her that

William was the only chance of survival she had. But would he save her from death or help her on her way with a push? Either way could mean death. But Elizabeth would rather die accidentally than give William the satisfaction of ending her life.

But maybe he'll save you!

A part of Elizabeth wanted to believe it until she thought back to the moments before she had fallen. No. She *couldn't* believe him, not now. If she just let herself go, she would die free.

But then William's face would be the last she'd ever see. He had been right when he'd said that he was her destiny. If it weren't for him, she wouldn't be here now, just seconds away from death.

Yes, even after his death, William had hunted Elizabeth down like an animal. And now he would share her last breath before her fate was sealed in blood.

"Who . . . what . . . are you?" Tom shrank back from the woman in his arms, shaking with bewilderment and shock. The "face" that greeted him was anything but familiar, for it was not even a face. Framed by thick, golden hair was nothing but a blank, white void. No face at all—and certainly not the heart-shaped face of the fantasy Elizabeth he'd cherished and dreamed about.

"B-But . . . ," he stammered, stepping away from the faceless girl nervously. *Is this some kind of horrible joke?* he wondered.

Turning his back to the princess, Tom tried to swallow his disappointment. But he felt horribly dismayed, as if he'd just lost something precious that could never be replaced.

And yet it made no sense! He'd thought he knew everything about the princess. He'd thought they were soul mates. And now . . . this? Nothing but a blank space where a face should be? Was that his princess? Was that his soul mate?

A hollow ache expanded in Tom's chest as he whirled around to face the girl again. Still no change. She stared at him . . . well, it wasn't as if she really could, seeing as how she had no eyes. Yet Tom felt as if she was confronting him, facing him, challenging him.

"You're not my fantasy," Tom said. "You're not my soul mate."

But if she *isn't, then who is?* an insidious voice whispered inside Tom's head.

"Not her!" Tom shouted, pointing at the faceless girl. "She's . . . she's *nothing!*"

As Tom's words echoed in the chamber, the princess's shoulders seemed to droop, and her chest appeared to sink. With a last shimmer of her golden hair she turned her head and dissolved into static.

"Ugh! That was awful!" Tom groaned. He threw down his headset and ran a shaking hand through his hair. He had a bad taste in his mouth, his head clanged like a gong, and his insides felt as if they'd been squeezed by an iron clamp. That faceless freak wasn't *supposed* to be Elizabeth . . . was it?

Disoriented and nauseous, Tom stumbled out of the tent. His mind felt as if it were on a roller coaster, and the world seemed to have been knocked off its axis—everything was lopsided, off balance, and shaky. Everything except one thing: Inside Tom's soul a small kernel of bitterness hardened into a stone and lodged itself. And Tom knew it would remain there for a very long time.

"Do it, Elizabeth! Take my hand!"

"So you can be the one to let me go?" Elizabeth retorted. She knew she couldn't hold on much longer. She was aware she was about to plummet to certain death. But she didn't want to give William the satisfaction of speeding things up.

"Elizabeth, I'll never let you go. You know that." William's eyes were large with fear, and his voice cracked. "I was only trying to scare you back there, but I never meant to harm you. You have to believe me."

Can I? Elizabeth bit her cheek so hard, she tasted blood. While Elizabeth hated the power William had over her, she knew that any hope she had of being saved lay with him and him alone.

Take his hand, she commanded herself, her muscles screaming for relief. She wouldn't be able to hold on much longer, and already she'd heard a dull snap as one of the roots she clung to gave out. *Do it!*

Hesitantly Elizabeth uncurled her left hand, feeling pain as blood began to circulate through it once more. Limply she held it out to him, never once taking her eyes off his. She was dealing with a man she could never trust, a man who transformed from loving to malevolent in seconds. Did he really believe he loved her, or was he just enjoying the way he was systematically ruining her life?

William grasped the tips of her fingers, and Elizabeth felt a second of terrible, sweeping doubt, a second that seemed to stretch into a lifetime. Would he pull or push?

His fingers brushed hers again. No. *No!* He was just toying with her!

But right when she thought it was over for her, Elizabeth felt William grasp her hand firmly and begin to pull.

And then it happened.

His foot slipped on a loose rock and he lost his balance. With a pained, wordless exclamation William let go of Elizabeth's hand to steady himself. But his foot slid out farther, and as if in slow motion Elizabeth saw William's body arc up and tumble over her head into thin air.

William screamed as he fell through the sky, his body little more than a tiny, dark speck below her against a great expanse of blue. As William's body reached the sand below, she closed her eyes, her entire body in a state of shock.

Elizabeth grasped the roots tighter and began

to cry. William *had* been her one and only chance for survival. And now he was gone.

He might as well have taken her with him. At least she wouldn't have had to die alone.

"Alison, Alison, Alison," Jessica drawled with a shake of her head. "So *you're* the one who's after *my* Jonah!"

"Oops! I *do* believe you're talking about *my* boyfriend, thank you very much," Alison sneered. "And—*sorry!*—there's nothing you can do about it."

Quicker than lightning, Jessica pulled the revolver from her belt and aimed it at Alison. She was beyond confused, but all she knew was that Alison Quinn had to be stopped. *Destroy now, questions later,* Jessica told herself, cocking the barrel of her gun.

"Jessica-a-a-a!" Alison whined. "Don't *do* this! I'm the Theta vice president, *rememberrr?*"

"Look. I don't know what you're up to, Quinn, but you won't get away with it," Jessica spat, pulling *her* Jonah to her side. "Nice of you to drop in on our CyberDream, but now it's time to make your exit. Jonah's mine, and you can kiss him good-bye—*figuratively,* I mean. Oh—and by the way, I'd be happy to tell you a little about the place I'm sending you to, OK? Hint: *No one cares about sorority rank!*"

"Stop!" Alison snarled. Jessica saw a flash of light and then realized that Alison had reached for her own gun. But it was too late for Jessica to stop her with a bullet. They were in a Mexican standoff, both aiming at each other, trigger fingers itching to fire.

"Looks like we're at a stalemate, Wakefield." Alison yanked the second Jonah toward her. "And I'll have you know for the record, Jonah's mine! I don't know what you're trying to pull here, but this is *my* CyberDream and *my* guy! So either go back to your own turf or die!"

As the two girls stared down the barrels of their guns, Jessica locked her jaw determinedly, trying to look cool and defiant even though her thoughts were whirling around like tumbleweed in a hurricane. Was she really in Alison's CyberDream? Or was Alison in hers? The whole thing was too confusing for Jessica, and frankly, she didn't feel like wasting another minute of her precious time over it. Arguing with Alison hardly fit Jessica's profile of the perfect CyberDream. She didn't care who was in whose dream. All she knew was that when it came to her men, she wasn't about to share.

Jessica smiled viciously at Alison and laid a possessive hand on Jonah's arm. "Tell her, Jonah," she ordered. "Go on, break her jealous heart. She needs to hear it from you."

"Hear what?" Jonah asked innocently.

Hello? Was this guy slower than a tortoise on Valium or what? Jessica glared at Jonah. He smiled back, apparently unperturbed by all the drama.

"Tell her you're with me!" she hissed.

"Tell *her* you're with *me!*" Alison repeated to the second Jonah.

Suddenly, right in front of Jessica's amazed eyes, both Jonahs morphed into one. "Girls, girls, girls," Jonah said with a smooth chuckle. "Why can't we all just . . . get along?"

"Gross!" Alison shrieked, still holding her gun on Jessica, although a bit more shakily.

"You traitor!" Jessica yelled, her firing arm wavering nervously.

"Two-timing slime!" Alison screamed.

"Disgusting pig!" Jessica cried.

"Hey, hey, relax!" Jonah held his hands up in a gesture of defeat. "We can be . . . *reasonable* about this, can't we?"

"Eew, no!" Jessica and Alison chorused.

"Come on, we can work this out," Jonah pleaded, flashing both women his most dazzling smile.

Jessica shook her head in disbelief. It was all too much to take in at once. None of it made any sense. But as Jessica regarded Jonah warily, she had a feeling that *he* knew *exactly* what was going on.

"Look, you two, there's no need to fight over me." Jonah licked his lips. "You can *both* have me. Know what I mean?"

Jessica and Alison shared an outraged look.

"Jeez, what a sleazebag!" Alison said.

"I know," Jessica agreed, her cheeks flaming like a torch. "And *he* thinks he's good enough to share?" Without hesitation she turned and trained her gun on Jonah. "I don't *think* so, mister!"

Alison did the exact same thing. "And if you think we're going to let you get away with this, you've just made your second mistake!"

Just as Jessica and Alison cocked their guns, everything turned to static.

"What was *that* all about?" Jessica complained as she took off her headset and flung it across the room. Her head was one big question mark. Meanwhile her body shook with rage and humiliation. She didn't know what was scarier—the fact that she and Alison had shared a CyberDream, a boyfriend, or an actual opinion. The notion of actually *agreeing* with the Simpleton of Sorority Row was pretty creepy, but perhaps not quite as creepy as the idea that Jonah had somehow manipulated both their minds in order to get his groove on in cyberspace. What a pathetic loser!

That slimy reptile sure has a lot of nerve, she thought, flouncing out of the cubicle. She'd thought Jonah was just a shy, skittish, yet unbelievably hot-looking science geek who didn't know how to behave with a woman one-on-one. She'd thought she could trust him. She'd thought this time would be different. But he was just a scheming loser like all the rest! The whole time she was behind the CyberDreams tent with him, he was probably keeping an eye out for Alison! *Eew!*

Although she still hadn't figured out quite the

whats, hows, and whys of the trick Jonah had tried to pull, Jessica knew a scam when she saw one. And once she had it figured out, she was going to make Jonah Falk pay. No one messed with Jessica Wakefield's heart *and* brain and expected to get away with it.

Chapter Fifteen

But I don't want to die! I'm not ready to die!

As Elizabeth clung to the edge of the cliff, an image of Jessica's face swam before her eyes, followed by Tom's, and then another and another until everyone she cared about jostled in her mind. She pictured everyone sobbing at her funeral, all the people she'd leave behind. And all because of William White! She couldn't let it happen. Not even in a CyberDream.

With almost superhuman strength Elizabeth clawed her way upward with her left hand, her nails on fire as she dug into dust and dry grass. Her muscles burned with exertion, but she forced herself to inch a little farther, adrenaline pumping fiercely through her veins. Now if she could just get her right hand to let go of the clump of roots and grab that rock . . .

Elizabeth took a deep breath. Beads of sweat

stung her eyes. She knew that saving herself would require a moment of ultimate terror—the moment when her right hand would have to let go. As she heard another root snap, she knew she had no choice. She was just seconds away from falling.

She let go and—

Yes! Elizabeth almost cried with relief as her right hand made contact with the rock. Just one more step to take. Slowly and with great deliberation she moved her other hand to the slab of granite. Now she was holding on to the edge of the cliff with a firm enough grip to pull herself up and over . . . to safety. And she did.

Elizabeth wept as she lay in the soft grass. Her brush with death had been so close that all she could do was savor the feeling of being alive.

After a few minutes Elizabeth sat up. She was still elated by her escape, but something was pressing down on her . . . something that threatened to destroy her sense of victory.

Maybe it's not all over, she thought fearfully. *Maybe William isn't really dead!*

And then Elizabeth laughed. A dry, mirthless laugh. This was just like seeing him in the aftermath of the car wreck. There was no way he could be alive because *she had just watched him die.* No one could survive a fall like that, just like no one could survive a car accident with such massive injuries.

No one except William, her inner voice whispered.

Elizabeth bit her lip. He *had* faked his own

death before. But how could this one possibly be faked? There was only one way to find out.

Quickly she scanned the steep cliff, looking for a way down. Finding a rocky but navigable path down to the beach, she followed it. At times she had to half slide her way down, but Elizabeth was on a mission. She had to see William's body for herself.

This is going to be ugly, she warned herself as her feet finally made contact with sand. But she had to do it. It was the only way to be sure he was dead.

Slowly Elizabeth walked to the far side of the curving bay to the spot where William would have landed. To her right the sand cast a blinding white glare and to her left the navy blue sea lapped gently at the tide line. Any other time Elizabeth would have welcomed such a beautiful, undisturbed natural landscape, but at that moment it made her feel even more frightened. The emptiness of the long, deserted beach together with the brilliant light of the sun gave her a feeling of despair and foreboding.

The emptiness.

Of course.

In the place where William's body should have been, there was nothing but an open stretch of sand. Not even an imprint disturbed the large expanse of white. It was untouched. No one had walked there, let alone fallen from the cliff and landed there.

Elizabeth dropped to her knees, dizzy from terror. The hot sun beat down on her forehead unforgivingly.

"He's not dead," she cried, a terrified whimper escaping from her lips. "He's never going to die. Never . . ."

She began to feel delirious as the white sand gleamed, filling her vision with a hot, blinding light that blotted out everything else. Elizabeth saw nothing but whiteness and heard nothing but the sound of her own sobs. She knew she'd be seeing William again soon, hearing that familiar voice telling her he'd never leave her. . . .

Suddenly Elizabeth realized she was shaking in her cubicle, slumped to the ground, the headset around her neck. Even slipping the headset down had required an effort she hadn't felt capable of in her weak, frightened state.

The dream had not gone as she'd planned. It had ended with a question mark. Just the way William would have wanted it to.

And now for the life of her, Elizabeth couldn't see how she'd ever be sure she was truly rid of William White. It certainly looked as if his ghost would haunt her forever, locked inside her mind, strewing rose petals through not just her worst nightmares, but through her every waking moment.

Tom shuddered as he left the tent, trying to block the ghostly white sheets from his view. Their blank whiteness only reinforced the creepy image in his mind of the blank, white void in place of the face that should have been there.

What does all this mean? The question raged inside Tom, burning a hole through his skull and fueling the despair he felt deep inside. If he was supposed to be cyberdreaming of Elizabeth, then what did that white void represent?

Is she really a stranger to me? he thought, horrified. *Do I really* not *know the woman I love?*

That seemed to be the only logical interpretation. Tom shuddered to think of its ramifications. His faceless Elizabeth, unrecognizable, a complete mystery, and yet . . . his fantasy? Obviously deep down, he had been feeling more and more unconnected to Elizabeth as of late. After all their time together, she was still a mystery to him. Maybe he didn't love her as much as he thought he did . . . or maybe it was the other way around.

Shattered, Tom walked almost without knowing where he was going, feeling as if his entire world had been blown into a million tiny pieces. His rock-solid relationship was nothing but a sham. He'd been living in a fantasyland for who knew how long. And it took a CyberDream—no, make that *three* CyberDreams—for him to see it!

He almost laughed out loud. It would have been poetic if it weren't so pathetic. His life with Elizabeth—everything he'd believed in and felt secure in—was just an illusion.

"I thought we had trust!"

Tom looked up to see Lila, her face red with anger, hollering at Bruce, who looked like an atomic explosion just waiting to happen.

"That's *rich* coming from you!" Bruce bellowed. "This relationship is obviously a total lie!"

I can relate to that, Tom thought sadly, bowing his head as an image of Elizabeth came to mind. It was Elizabeth, all right—her long blond hair and slender, graceful figure. But right now Tom couldn't picture her face. It just swirled in front of his eyes, vague, undefined—a blank, white oval. . . .

"You went behind my back and cyberdreamed when you *knew* it was bad for you!" Lila's voice shook with rage, her eyes flashing with hurt and betrayal.

"You're missing something here, Lila." Bruce glared at her, arms folded. "Before you get on your high horse and act like you're so innocent, you should take a long, hard look at yourself! *You* also promised not to cyberdream, and there you were!"

"That's hardly the same thing," Lila retorted. "I lied because I knew if I told you I would go, you'd want to go too. But *I* wasn't the one in danger here! *You* couldn't handle *your* CyberDreams! Let me remind you who got beat up last night because he was too busy thinking he was Jean-Claude Van Damme!"

"Stop trying to slime your way out of this, Li," Bruce shot back, his voice rising in frustration. "You *still* lied. We both did!"

"Look, Bruce," she spat. "You've been *totally* self-absorbed ever since you tried that dream machine, so how can you blame me for wanting to be with the virtual Bruce? I hardly recognize you these days. All you care about is where your next thrill is coming from. So when I need some attention, I have to go into cyberspace to get it!"

"Well," Bruce countered, "maybe if you didn't expect so much of me, then I wouldn't feel I had to prove myself to you all the time!" He stared at Lila, bitterness in his eyes. "It's all *your* fault I went back and had a terrible dream, you know."

Lila turned away, feeling tears of frustration spring to her eyes. "You weren't the *only* one who had a bad trip, Bruce," she reminded him, her voice low and small. "You were just *awful* to me in my dream—just awful!" Lila hiccuped as a sob rose in her throat. The memory of Bruce trying to pay her for spending the night with him was more than she could bear.

"Li, please stop crying." Bruce's voice was gentle, and he moved tentatively toward her. "Don't you see? This has gotten way out of control. We're arguing over some dumb game, and now we're letting it destroy our relationship. *We* are real—the rest was just . . . stupid!"

Lila stopped midsob and frowned. What Bruce

was saying made sense. "You're right," she exclaimed. "We're letting CyberDreams get between us, and they're not even real."

"Our love is real," Bruce murmured. He pulled Lila into his arms and kissed her shoulder. "And no dopey virtual reality . . . *thing* can change what we feel for each other."

"So you don't think I'm a . . . *lady of the night?*" Lila joked, although inside she still felt a tremor of uncertainty. The dream had just seemed so real.

"I'm not even going to answer that," Bruce replied, running a hand through Lila's hair. "And in case you have another question, I'll answer it now: No, I would *never* let you blow up. I love you way too much."

"Well, I have to admit, you did look kind of cute when you faced up to those muggers last night." Lila smiled coyly.

"I was only doing what I had to," Bruce replied, his chest swelling with pride.

Uh-oh! Lila told herself to get a grip—and fast. One more step on this conversation trail and she'd have *Batman,* not Patman, for a boyfriend again. And she was perfectly happy with Patman. Really.

"Now, now," she said teasingly, "no need to get all puffed up. I know you weren't trying to defend me last night. You were only trying to prove your strength."

"But—"

"Shhh!" Lila put a finger to Bruce's bruised lips. "That silly stuff is behind us. I like you the way you are, remember? No more tough-guy stuff. You're Bruce *Patman,* not Bruce *Willis.*"

Bruce tightened his arms around her. "You really like me the way I am?"

Lila snuggled against his chest. "Of course I do." She sighed with relief. "We were so dumb to let those stupid dreams control our lives, you know," she murmured, wrapping her arms around his waist.

"Yeah," Bruce agreed. "Hey, you know what? I actually feel pretty good right now."

"And why is that?"

"Because I have you, sweetheart." Bruce kissed Lila softly on the forehead.

"Mmmm. I liked that." She stroked his cheek gently, thrilled to be making up the old-fashioned way. No money involved. Right now there was only one thing she wanted, and money couldn't buy it.

Lila got her wish as Bruce tilted her chin and gave her the kiss of her dreams. *The kiss of my* life, Lila corrected herself. After all, happiness was in the here and now, and it was free. Fantasies were just for the unlucky fools who didn't have true love.

"*You* are the *lowest* of the *low,*" Jessica spat, staring down at Jonah as he cowered in his chair and held out his arms, defenseless, in his tiny, makeshift "office." Not very impressive—just a small sheeted space with a cheap desk and a folding chair. Tacky, tacky, tacky. Jessica thought back to the spacious, beautifully furnished quarters she'd enjoyed as Jessica Wakefield, PI—

Enough! she chided herself, forcing the dream away. Dreams had gotten her into enough trouble. Now it was time to deal with reality. "I need answers," she snapped, glaring at Jonah, who looked as if he wanted to run away and disappear into cyberspace forever.

"That makes two of us!" Alison strode into the office with her hands on her hips. "Jessica, I have a feeling that you and I had the exact same CyberDream!"

"Mmm-hmm."

"So how do you explain *that,* Mr. Each Dream Is Unique?"

"I, uh . . ." Jonah hemmed, hawed, and looked sheepish.

"You messed with our minds, didn't you?" Jessica accused, her eyes boring into Jonah's. "You sick, twisted—"

"Well . . ." Jonah trailed off and looked at the ground.

"Coward!" Jessica yelled. "You don't even have the guts to admit it!"

"And it is so totally obvious that you did *something,*" Alison added. "Or else we wouldn't be here, would we?" Her voice dripped with sarcasm, and she crossed the floor to stare Jonah full in the face. "How dare you manipulate us like—like—like cheap pieces of trash."

Jessica raised an eyebrow.

"You should be prosecuted for this!" Alison continued, undaunted. "You should be sent up the river without a paddle or something!"

"OK, OK," Jonah replied, sighing. "I guess you have a right to be mad. I *did* go into the system and mess with your dreams."

He briefly pulled back a curtain, revealing a massive computer system. On the floor lay an individual headset, which Jonah must have worn while he insinuated himself into Jessica's and Alison's CyberDreams.

"I just wanted to try and get with one—or both—of you. OK?" Jonah explained. "Because, well . . . I'm not that great with girls in real life. I guess you already knew that, Jessica. You know, that time behind the tent?"

"*What?* You—you—," Alison spluttered while Jessica took a moment to look smug.

Jonah looked at the ground. "But then your minds combined kind of overtook mine . . . and, well, even with the whole system at my disposal, I couldn't manipulate your dreams to get what I wanted. I apologize to you both. Really. It was a pretty cheap and underhanded thing to do. And, well, I guess it was disgusting too." He lifted his head and shot them both a wicked smile. "But hey, I couldn't resist!"

"Of all the lowest, *lamest* pickup schemes . . . ," Jessica growled.

"I know." Jonah sighed, looking up at her with a forlorn, puppy-dog expression in his big, coal black eyes. "But try to see it this way: I gave you both what you wanted. It's kind of flattering when you think about it. . . ."

"Flattering? Are you *serious?"* Jessica fumed. "You make us share a CyberDream, play us like we're characters in your own sick fantasy, and we're supposed to be *flattered?* You're ten cents short of a dime there, buddy! I mean, first of all, Alison and I don't even *like* each other—"

"That's right," Alison chimed in.

"Jessica, Alison, please. Try to understand! I think—"

"*Hel*-lo!" Jessica held up her hand, silencing Jonah. "Who *cares* what you think? I suggest you let go of your headset and go get your head *read!* Or at least go buy yourself some Viagra or something!" Her eyes flashing, Jessica flared her nostrils angrily and marched out of the office.

I'm through with men! she thought, seething as she stormed through the tent. And she was *especially* through with lame-o mystery men like Jonah. If a man had an air of mystery about him, obviously it meant only one thing: He was hiding something she did *not* want to know about.

"Jessica, wait up!" Alison called out breathlessly as she struggled to catch up with her. "You were great in there. I really think together we gave him something to chew on."

"Hmpph!" Jessica could only grunt as Alison went on. All she wanted to do was go to her dorm room and nurse her wounds. The last thing she wanted right now was to contend with Alison sucking up to her like they should be called the Superfriends or the Bestest Buddies.

"Listen, Jessica, I've been thinking. There doesn't have to be all this tension between us, you know. It's, like, really dumb? So I think we should try to be friends," Alison continued in a syrupy voice. "I mean, if you think about it, we have tons in common! Truce?"

Tons in common? Jessica wondered. Yeah, right. They were both taken for a ride by the same moron—gee, those were grounds for an everlasting friendship! Sure, Alison might have helped Jessica dump on Jonah, but that was about all she was good for, in Jessica's opinion. She wouldn't even trust that woman with her laundry, let alone her friendship.

". . . and we're both popular and we're in the same sorority," Alison cooed. "There's just *so* much similarity between you and me. It'd be a shame to let that, like, go to waste. *Hmmm?*"

Wrong! Jessica was mortified. If Alison thought she could even come close to trespassing Jessica's orbit, she was deluding herself in a major way. Aside from being competitive and sneaky, Alison was a slimy, prissy snot with bad taste in clothes and damaged, shine-free hair. Not exactly suited to be a hanger-on in Jessica's chic circle. Maybe Jessica would consider tolerating her every so often, but friends? Alison weaseling her way into Jessica's scene and Jessica's closet? *Not in this lifetime!*

"Uh, Alison, I really have to be somewhere right now," Jessica cut her off brusquely. "See you around," she added as Alison raised her eyebrows, clearly miffed by the brush-off.

"Ugh! What a weekend," Jessica groaned as she made her way to Dickenson. First the man of her dreams turned out to be a nightmare, and then her absolute *worst* nightmare of a sorority sister suddenly wanted her stamp of approval. Beyond gross. The moment Jessica hit the second floor of Dickenson Hall, she was heading for a hot shower—with bleach, preferably, so she could scrub the entire icky weekend right out of her skin.

But you aren't seeing the reality! Elizabeth chided herself. She was still partially in a daze, sitting on the ground in her cubicle like a stupefied wreck. But part of her was lucid, shouting at the other half to get it together.

For the last ten minutes Elizabeth had been fretting, convinced that somehow, because William's body had mysteriously disappeared from the beach, that meant he was still alive. But little by little she began to see things in a new light, began to read the symbolism differently, more optimistically. Perhaps he wasn't there because he really *was* gone—forever. Yes, *that* was what her CyberDream was really trying to tell her.

All at once Elizabeth felt a rush of relief bring her numbed body back to life. Dreams had to be interpreted. They weren't logical, like real life, but they could be figured out easily enough. And if ever there was a sign that William's ghost had left her psyche once and for all, his missing body had to be it.

Elizabeth felt as if she'd just been resuscitated after drowning or as if she'd just found the last stray piece of a puzzle. Everything had taken shape, and the picture was finally clear. Just like an actual lucid dream, Elizabeth's CyberDream had obeyed her in the end. She had stood fast and faced her demon, and she had triumphed. She had driven her demon away for good.

Elizabeth took a deep breath and sighed. It had been a terrible ordeal, but she'd done her best to come through it. *And I have,* she told herself. *At least, I* think *I have. . . .*

William White, like any true psychotic, had always been full of surprises, and his sly, wily nature had always kept her guessing. But even if absolute certainty eluded her now, Elizabeth was sure that by morning, when the fair was over and done with, she'd accept once and for all that William White was dead and never coming back. After all, William *had* only appeared in her CyberDreams. She'd thought she'd seen him on the quad and at her window, but she'd only ever seen him in her dreams. And her dreams were merely a product of her imagination. . . . *Which means that ultimately I'm still the boss,* Elizabeth concluded. And now she'd finally put an end to it all.

"Hey, Jonah?"

Elizabeth stiffened. The voice belonged to Tom, and it came directly from the other side of her sheeted cubicle entrance.

"Can I talk to you for a sec?" Tom continued. "I just have a quick question about—"

"OK, whatever," Jonah replied. "Follow me. My office is over here. . . ."

Elizabeth kept dead still in her booth, her mind ticking wildly. She had to get out of there before Tom caught her. CyberDreams had done enough damage to her relationship, and if Tom knew she had lied, it would be a disaster.

As she made a break for it and ran unseen from the tent, Elizabeth sensed that she was finally leaving her troubled past behind her for good. *So long, CyberDreams,* she called silently. *Please* don't *come back anytime soon!*

Chapter Sixteen

"As you can see, I had a pretty weird experience with your equipment," Tom intoned as Jonah listened quietly. "I'm not asking for my money back, and I know you don't guarantee that the third dream will be a good one, but I need to understand how this works."

"Sorry, guy. I'm afraid we can't give out technical information," Jonah replied smoothly.

Tom silenced him with a tired look. "Off the record," he replied. "Please. It's really important to me."

Jonah folded his arms, leaning back until his chair rocked. "I'm sorry, Tom, but no can do. We have to protect our trade."

"And I have to protect my rights!" Tom yelled, shaking his fist. "You people come here and think you can do exactly what you like. But I'll have you know that I'm a reporter, and I can and will expose you on television if I have to. I may not be able to do much more than give you a lot of bad press, but that could be pretty harmful to your so-called business!"

Jonah swallowed, evidently impressed by Tom's threat. "All right. I'll tell you. If we can keep this between us."

"Fine."

"Remember what I told you about each dream being individual? That's not true. CyberDreams are fake, preprogrammed fantasies. We have several stock CyberDreams running through our machines, so we just take a close look at each dreamer and . . . guess which one will work."

"Guess?" Tom exploded.

Jonah nodded, a wry smile at his lips. "It's not too hard. Bruce Patman, for instance—rich, macho frat boy. It doesn't take a rocket scientist to match him up with a James Bond–style CyberDream. And how about you? I remember now. I took one look at you on Friday night, with your arms wrapped around your girlfriend like you were trying to keep her from being sucked off the face of the earth, and I instantly knew you saw yourself as the knight-in-shining-armor type."

"But—"

"I'm not done yet. There is *one* part of the process that does require the dreamer's imagination. The faces of the characters the dreamer encounters are left void. Each dreamer subconsciously fills in each important blank with the face of his or her dreams. It's pretty much foolproof—I mean, everyone has a fantasy."

"But I saw a void!" Tom shouted, confusion and anger welling up inside him like a tidal wave. "My princess had no face!"

"Sorry, man." Jonah shrugged. "Guess you just couldn't come up with a face to fit."

"That's ridiculous!" Tom spluttered, reddening. "I was supposed to be dreaming of my girlfriend—I *know* I was."

Jonah scratched his head, cool as a cucumber. "Hey, you don't have to convince me," he responded, smiling lazily. "Talk to your girlfriend, OK? *I'm* not upset that deep down inside, I'm not the face of your dreams."

"But I did dream about her!" Tom shook his head, trying to make sense of it all. If what Jonah was saying was true, then why did Tom, of all people, find it so hard to fill in the blank?

"Look, pal, don't blame me for this," Jonah said, waving Tom off. "I don't really know all the ins and outs of how the game works. I'm basically playing it by ear here. Some guy just hired me for this job, and it's what I do. All right? If you have a problem, I'm sorry, but it's not mine."

"I *do* have a problem," Tom interjected. "I think if you mess with people's minds, you should make sure your equipment is functioning!"

"I just take orders from my boss," Jonah retorted,

his voice cool and dispassionate. "Some weird guy, about our age, actually. He dreamed up this whole thing and he's loaded with cash, so I signed on. I'm no techie and I'm no psychologist, so I can't tell you more than I already have. I'm just the pitchman. That's all I am."

But Tom had long ago shut out Jonah's senseless excuses. "It *was* Elizabeth," he muttered, his mind spinning as he tried to figure out what had gone wrong. "It was *supposed* to be Elizabeth. I know it was."

"Elizabeth Wakefield?" Jonah asked, breaking Tom's concentration.

"You know her?" Tom was shocked. "How did you guess?"

"Sure. She's, uh, well, I *think* she's the only person left inside," Jonah replied hesitantly. "See?" He pointed to his sign-in sheet.

"Elizabeth is *here?*" Tom was dumbfounded. *She snuck in behind my back!* Tom could hardly believe it. Not only was it difficult to swallow Elizabeth's lying to him, but to think she had the stupidity to go for a third dose of CyberDreams when the first two had made her freak out! *I guess I* don't *know my girlfriend after all,* Tom lamented as he strode back into the tent and checked each cubicle.

She was gone, but Tom was determined to find her. He dashed out of the tent and scanned the quad. But Elizabeth was nowhere to be seen. *She couldn't have gotten* that *far,* Tom reasoned. *Wait—there she is!*

His eyes tracked the figure of Elizabeth, who could just barely be seen through the branches of scattered trees in the distance. She was running up a hill on the edge of the quad, near the WSVU building.

Tom broke into a sprint, determined to catch up with her and give her a piece of his mind. He picked up the pace as his fury rose, his mind an angry mass of splintered emotions and unanswered questions knotted together by an overall sense of betrayal. "Elizabeth!" he shouted, his voice hoarse as he watched her speeding up the hill, running like a madwoman.

Crack!

A sharp pain shot through Tom's head, resonating like a cymbal's crash. He stumbled and half turned to see where the blow had come from. But he never got that far. A searing, stinging cloak engulfed his entire head and his vision blurred as he staggered forward.

"Eliz—," he croaked, falling to his knees. The grass rose to meet him. And everything went from green to black.

"Tom?" Elizabeth whirled around and then frowned. "Tom? Was that you?" She could have sworn she'd heard Tom calling her name, but she didn't see him anywhere.

Suddenly Elizabeth's mouth dropped like an anchor and stayed just as still. From her vantage point at the top of the hill, she could see the entire quad. In the short time it had taken her to run from the tent to the hill, the sky had cleared to a perfect robin's egg blue, the dark clouds had scattered away, and the sun had come out. But most bizarrely of all, the CyberDreams tent had disappeared. It was gone.

She could only blink and stare, gaping at the place on the lawn where the tent should have been. Was her mind playing tricks on her again? She squinted, then widened her eyes warily. The tent was gone, all right. Not a trace of it remained.

Into thin air! Elizabeth thought, shaking her head in bewilderment. Nothing but green grass and students milling around like any other normal day on campus. No white sheets, no purple sky, no gloomy, dark clouds or ghostly, white rosebud logo. It was as if the Virtual Reality Fair—*and* the entire weekend—had never happened.

Elizabeth couldn't even begin to fathom what she was seeing—or not seeing. How could the tent have simply disappeared? *I must be going crazy,* she told herself. But she sure didn't *feel* crazy. If anything, she felt completely . . . *normal.*

As Elizabeth slowly descended the hill, she felt

something growing inside her with each step. Something familiar . . .

Me! Elizabeth smiled tremulously. It was strange and amazing, but she felt as if the clock had suddenly turned back a few days. Back to when everything had been normal, typical problems like relationships and finals dominating everyone's minds. Back when CyberDreams fever hadn't turned everyone into crazed cyberjunkies, jostling each other in line and blabbering about their fantasies.

Maybe it was all just a dream . . . or a nightmare!

Maybe none of it really happened!

Why else would I fantasize about William White?

Elizabeth's mind teemed with questions, but soon she found she could address each one firmly and calmly, just like she normally could. No more panicking. No more crazy, paranoid conclusions. She felt like Elizabeth Wakefield again, dedicated student and patient journalist, fact checking everything to its minute details. She didn't have all the answers, but she had a few theories.

First of all, there was the weird weather: a strange, eerie storm that no one had foreseen and no one could explain. Could it be that what had happened was something beyond ordinary science? A strange twilight-zone kind of weather phenomenon that had somehow played with Elizabeth's brain and given her an otherworldly, paranormal take on whatever she experienced? Or perhaps the weather had acted as a strangely powerful sedative, propelling her into a kind of dream state where she'd hallucinated the entire weekend's events? *Not likely,* Elizabeth reasoned, her skeptical side kicking in.

But logic still couldn't explain what had happened, and Elizabeth still felt perplexed as she made her way down the hill. Although she liked her own weird and wacky theories, she preferred an explanation that lay within the bounds of convention and reality. Twilight zone and *X-Files* phenomena were not really possibilities that Elizabeth could believe in, no matter how much she wished she could. It had to be something else.

Maybe they just packed up the tent really fast, and I was too lost in thought to notice the passing of time. That was plausible. *Or maybe the tent is still there and making it disappear is just some kind of carnival trick, done with mirrors or something.* Although the quad sure looked empty from afar, the second theory could also be true, especially since it was the fair's last day. *Maybe this is their big finale, their trademark finish. . . .*

And then, quite unexpectedly, Elizabeth found herself at an unusual point in her thinking. With all the possibilities piling up in her head like a stack of playing cards, she suddenly realized that she simply didn't care anymore. And it gave her the most liberating feeling. Whatever the explanations, whatever the truth, Elizabeth no longer felt any desire to break it all down and analyze it. It was as if the deck of cards were spread all around her mind and instead of looking at the numbers, Elizabeth had picked the joker. She didn't want any part of adding up numbers and matching suits. All she wanted was to get back to her normal life and move on.

Elizabeth smiled as she noticed a last wispy gray cloud floating away from the sun. The fear and paranoia that had clutched her heart for days had drifted away with it.

I'll never complain of boredom again, Elizabeth thought, chuckling as she remembered how dissatisfied she'd felt only a few days before. It seemed like an eternity ago. She vowed to appreciate what she had—especially with Tom. After all the tempestuousness that had rocked her weekend, Elizabeth had a newfound appreciation for her safe, secure relationship.

A warm glow of love touched her heart. She couldn't wait to find Tom and tell him how much his love meant to her. In a strange way, the weird weekend had done her a world of good. She knew what she had now and was never going to take it for granted again.

Elizabeth felt a gentle tap on her shoulder, and

she grinned. It was as if a genie had just granted her a wish. Elizabeth spun around, her smile lighting up as she anticipated the loving brown eyes she knew so well.

Her smile froze and died on her lips. The eyes were ice blue.

Elizabeth gasped and jumped back. Yes, there he stood before her.

William White.

A ray of brilliant sun shone down on him, illuminating the left side of his face, plunging the right into shadow. The sun turned his hair a brilliant golden white and made his eyes dance like sapphires. He looked so handsome, Elizabeth thought she was staring at an apparition. *Please let him be one,* she begged silently, praying that she was only having another strange, hallucinating spell.

William simply held out a white rosebud and stared deeply into Elizabeth's eyes. Her mind went blank. She accepted the rose numbly.

He can't be real, she thought. *I must still be cyberdreaming.*

But as she took the flower by its stem, a thorn pricked her index finger, sending a needle of pain darting through her hand and into her forearm. The pain felt real.

Wordlessly Elizabeth stared at her finger. A bead of blood dotted its tip. The blood looked real.

Instinctively she brought the finger to her lips. It tasted real too.

And all the while William White just stood there, smiling, his face half plunged in shadow. This was no hallucination, no trick of the eye. William White was real.

He was still alive.

William White desperately wants Elizabeth Wakefield's love and forgiveness—and he's doing everything he can to show her how much he's changed. But has he changed for better or for worse? Find out in the conclusion to this block-buster two-part Sweet Valley University Thriller Edition, **DEADLY TERROR: THE RETURN OF WILLIAM WHITE, PART II.**